Lucas wasn't aware he'd dozed off until he woke up with a start

Miranda was snuggled against him on the couch. She slept fitfully, her forehead creased. Her hair tumbled in disarray around her shoulders. She murmured something in her sleep.

Unable to resist, he reached down and caressed her cheek.

She sighed, and the tension in her face relaxed. In spite of her reputation as a rough-and-tumble cowgirl, she felt soft and feminine beneath his hand, her body warm.

If only things could be different....

They *had* to find Miranda's sister. He wouldn't rest until they did.

Dear Reader,

The world is full of strong women, many of them single moms. Miranda Ward was raised by such a woman and, like her mother, she's learned to stand up for herself. That's why she didn't fall apart when Lucas Blaylock left her standing at the altar at the tender age of twenty. Miranda went on with her life, opening her own horse-training business, never dreaming she'd ever come to depend on Lucas for anything.

But when her sister, Shannon, disappears, Miranda has no choice but to turn to the man who is now the sheriff of Sage Bend, Montana, the man who once broke her heart. She'll do whatever it takes to find her sister and bring her home safely, and if that means counting on Lucas, so be it.

Lucas has risen above the roots of the abusive childhood he once knew to become a lawman. He takes pride in his job and all it stands for. He's not proud, however, of what he did to Miranda seven years ago—even though he still feels it was best for her. Now he has a chance to help her find her sister, and he won't rest until he brings Shannon Ward home. He just wishes there was something he could do to make Miranda see things his way.

Find out how two people overcome their past to find their future. I hope you enjoy the journey Miranda and Lucas take in their quest for a forever kind of love. Something neither has known before.

Happy reading!

Brenda Mott

THE SHERIFF
OF SAGE BEND
Brenda Mott

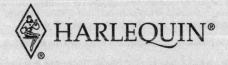

HARLEQUIN®

TORONTO • NEW YORK • LONDON
AMSTERDAM • PARIS • SYDNEY • HAMBURG
STOCKHOLM • ATHENS • TOKYO • MILAN • MADRID
PRAGUE • WARSAW • BUDAPEST • AUCKLAND

ISBN-13: 978-0-373-71430-8
ISBN-10:   0-373-71430-0

THE SHERIFF OF SAGE BEND

ABOUT THE AUTHOR

Brenda Mott grew up loving horses and books. She wrote her first short story at the age of nine, and from that point on was determined to be an author. In the early '80s she combined her two passions and penned several nonfiction magazine articles for various equine publications. She now happily writes for Harlequin Superromance, and her stories often reflect her love of horses. She enjoys writing romance, because there's always a guaranteed happy ending. Brenda lives in Tennessee with her husband, David, on a small ranch where they raise horses and take in every stray dog that happens by.

Books by Brenda Mott

HARLEQUIN SUPERROMANCE

This book is dedicated to all the strong women out there who have risen above whatever obstacles have come their way. And to the women who are not so strong, who do the best they can with the situations life has thrown them. Godspeed.

And with special acknowledgment and thanks to two of the strongest women I know: my editor, Victoria Curran, and my agent, Michelle Grajkowski.

CHAPTER ONE

"YOU HAVEN'T BEEN yourself lately, Shannon." Miranda Ward studied her sister's drawn expression. "What's wrong?"

"Nothing." Shannon feigned grave interest in her reflection as she swept her black hair into a ponytail and tied it with a scrunchie that had seen better days. "Can't a person want a little time alone without something being wrong?" She turned to face Miranda in the riding stable's tiny bathroom, nearly colliding with her.

"I know you better than that." Her sister stepped out of the way. "But if you don't want to tell me what it is, I guess I can't make you."

Shannon brushed past her, moving through their mother's office and on into the barn. "I'm going riding," she said. "We'll talk when I get back, okay?"

"Come on, let me go with you. Chet and Sam can hold the fort until Mom gets back from the feed store."

"Nope. Thanks anyway." Shannon waved over her shoulder as she headed for a nearby stall.

Undeterred, Miranda watched while her sister saddled her big bay gelding, Poker. "I was hoping you'd tell me about that phone call you got last night."

Shannon whirled back to her. "You were listening?" Her gaze darted to where Chet and Sam stood outside, jaw jacking with a couple of tourists who'd just returned from a ride.

Miranda kept her voice low. "No. But I couldn't help overhear some from Mom's living room. Did it have to do with the trial?"

Shannon's eyes widened briefly, and Miranda easily caught the nervousness her younger sister tried to hide. "What did you hear?"

"Nothing, really. Just you—on the phone. Who were you talking to at eleven o'clock?"

"None of your business."

That might be true—if Shannon wasn't a key witness in an upcoming rape and murder trial. "All right," Miranda finally said. "You want to have supper with me tonight?"

"Sure. If you promise not to interrogate me. I'll get enough of that when we go to court."

"I thought you said we'd talk later."

"And we will." Shannon led Poker down the aisle toward the open double doors at the far end. "See you."

"Have a good ride." Miranda watched as Shannon swung into the saddle and set off at a trot.

Poker's shod hooves clacked along the hard-packed dirt trail that wound through the scrub oak, growing fainter as he and Shannon turned off the main path and disappeared into the trees.

THIRTY MINUTES LATER, Miranda helped her mother unload the sweet feed from the pickup, glad for the chance to talk to her in private. Chet and Sam had taken a group of eight out on a trail ride minutes ago, heading north across Paige Ward's sixty-five acres. They'd be gone for at least an hour. Miranda tugged a fifty pound sack of grain toward the edge of the dropped tailgate. "Have you noticed anything wrong with Shannon lately, Mom? I know she's got a lot on her mind, but she's awfully withdrawn."

Paige paused, brushing her black bangs out of her eyes. Her dark Cherokee skin was further browned by the late June sun. People said Miranda looked more like her mother than Shannon did, even if Miranda's hair was brown and her eyes blue.

"The trial's got her out of sorts. Can't say as it hasn't left me with a few sleepless nights."

"Me, too. I'll be glad when it's over." Miranda shouldered the bag. "Shannon's been holding up pretty good through it all, though. Haven't you noticed it's only lately she's been acting weird? She didn't want me to go riding with her. And she was talking to someone on the phone late last night when I left the house."

"Is that a crime?" Paige hopped down from the truck and hefted a sack onto her own shoulder.

"No. But it's not like her." Miranda followed her into the barn. "And she hasn't been eating well lately, either."

Paige leaned the grain on the edge of a bulk-size feed bin. Overhead, swallows scolded from a mud nest in the rafters, then swooped away. "That's true enough. But you know how it is when you get busy. Sometimes I forget to eat, too."

"I wish I had that problem." Miranda pulled the string on the bag of feed, and sweet-smelling, molasses-covered oats, corn and milo poured in a golden arc into the bin. As she discarded the empty sack, she heard hoofbeats outside. "Sounds like Shannon's back."

"Well, that was a short ride. Maybe she decided to let you tag along, after all." Paige headed back to the truck.

"Yeah." Miranda walked to the rear doors, freezing as she looked out, her heart racing. "Mom! Come quick."

Poker galloped into the stable yard, riderless, stirrups flapping. Sweat soaked his coat, and his nostrils flared. "Whoa, boy." Miranda grabbed his dangling reins. One was broken, the leather snapped in two where he'd likely stepped on it. Poker's ears swiveled back and forth. Trembling, he dipped his head and blew loudly.

"What the hell…?"

"My God," Paige said from behind her, reaching

out to rest her hand on Poker's neck. "What happened? He's hotter than a firecracker."

Miranda's stomach pitched. "Shannon wouldn't do that to him on purpose." She looked at the saddle and caught her breath. "Mom." She touched the pommel, then looked down at her fingers. Blood.

"Oh, dear Lord." Paige's hand went to her chest. "Sam said he heard a cougar out back last night." There were hundreds of acres of public forest around Paige's riding stable, handled by the Bureau of Land Management.

Miranda shoved the gelding's reins at her. "Take him. I'm going to look for Shannon."

Paige calmed the riled horse. "I'll lock up and ride out with you."

"No, stay here. Call the sheriff's office." Wishing her roping horse wasn't several miles away at her own ranch, Miranda saddled Sundae, one of the best wrangler horses her mom owned—a big red dun. Her fingers flew as she threaded the latigo through the cinch and quickly tied it off.

She was shaking from head to toe.

Any rider could get bucked off, no matter how experienced. And accidents happened. The blood didn't necessarily point to a cougar attack. So what did it mean? Shannon wouldn't have passed by Sam and Chet and their group, because she'd headed up the east fork of the trail, so riding out to find them would do no good.

Where was she?

"Take the pistol," Paige said. "I'll get it." She hurried away, then returned with a holstered .44 and a set of saddlebags.

Miranda flung the bags behind the cantle, then slid the gun inside, queasy at the sight of her sister's blood on her hand. She grimaced and wiped her palm down the leg of her jeans.

Adrenaline on overload, she rode away at a gallop.

WHEN LUCAS BLAYLOCK HEARD the call come in over his police radio, his first impression was that Miranda Ward had been injured. His heart nearly leaped from his chest.

Miranda. A tough woman who'd never needed anyone. Least of all him.

Not since he'd left her standing at the altar seven years ago.

Flipping on his lights and siren, he turned his Chevy Blazer in a tight U and sped down the county road that led away from Sage Bend to the Rocking W. Shannon and Miranda were as close to each other as sisters could be, and he could imagine how worried Miranda and Paige were. A mountain lion had been reported in the vicinity, stalking cattle. But it wasn't only four-legged predators Lucas was thinking about.

Six months ago, a young woman—Jo Ella Jamison—had disappeared from the parking lot of the local honky-tonk. Her body had been found days later in the next county, stuffed in a culvert. Stripped. Raped.

And Shannon Ward was a key witness to the events preceding Jo Ella's murder.

Lucas pressed harder on the accelerator, and the high-powered engine responded, sending a plume of dust and gravel in the Chevy's wake.

Paige Ward met him in the driveway outside the barn, near where a bay gelding stood tied to a hitching post—soaked with sweat. Paige's lined face was pinched, and she gave him a look that was half worry, half resentment. She appeared a great deal older than forty-eight. But then she'd had a hard life. Paige had been running the Rocking W since her girls were toddlers. Since their father skipped out on them.

Yet another worthless excuse of a man.

Of course, he shouldn't talk.

"Sheriff," Paige said. "Thanks for coming so quickly." But her hard gaze let him know she didn't like him any better now than she had seven years ago.

"What happened?" He pulled out his notepad and scratched the details in a shorthand only he could decipher as she explained.

His top deputy, Garrett Rutledge, pulled in and parked behind the Blazer.

Paige gestured toward the bay. "I didn't want to unsaddle him until you'd had a look."

Lucas ran his hand over the horse's neck, noting the

blood on the pommel. "You'd better cool him down. But see if you can pull that saddle off without disturbing things too much. Set it over there." He motioned.

She bristled. "I'm not stupid, Sheriff." She lifted her chin. "I've already got a horse saddled and waiting for you in the barn. Figured you'd want to have a look for Shannon yourself." Her tone let him know she'd saddle a horse for Satan himself if he could bring her daughter back safely. "Miranda said she rode up the east trail."

Lucas nodded. "Thanks." Tucking the notebook in the pocket of his Western shirt, he tugged the brim of his silver Stetson down over his eyes. Mostly to keep it from blowing off when he rode, but also to hide his own concern from Paige. Five years as the sheriff of Sage Bend had hardened him to violence, but murder was rare in his town. Hell, only 875 people lived here. Besides, he had a soft spot for Miranda and her little sister.

Always had. Always would.

He spoke to Garrett, who agreed to stay with Paige, then they headed for the barn. Inside, he gathered the reins of the gray Paige had readied, led the horse out and mounted.

"Sheriff."

He looked down at her, tightening his grip as the gelding shifted beneath him.

Paige shielded her eyes from the midmorning sun. "Please find her."

"I'll do my best, ma'am."

"Don't ma'am me, Lucas Blaylock. I'm not that damned old."

His lips twitched. "Only if you stop calling me 'Sheriff.' It's Lucas to you, Paige. Ma'am." He put his heels to the gray and took off up the trail.

He caught up with Miranda sooner than he'd expected. Somehow, he'd pictured her—a tough, bronc-breaking cowgirl—riding her horse hell-for-leather to her sister's rescue. Instead, she was scanning the ground as her horse walked. She looked over her shoulder at him.

"Lucas." She spoke his name with a kind of formality. Not as she'd once said it, when he'd held her and made love to her. "I thought you'd send your deputies out here."

"You know me better than that." He scowled. "Tell me what happened."

"Didn't Mom talk to you?"

"Yeah. But I wanna hear it from you."

"Why? Don't waste my time, Lucas. My sister's hurt." She continued studying the ground.

"How can you see anything with all those tracks? Speaking of which, where are Sam and Chet?"

"On a group ride. They went up the north fork." She gestured. "Shannon rode off in this direction. We don't normally take our guests this way, since it's a fairly rough ride."

The smattering of tracks showed that more than

one horse had passed by here time and again. But on closer inspection, Lucas realized only one set looked fresh. He assumed they belonged to the horse they were tracking.

Miranda pointed. "You can see where her horse came back—over there. He'd veered off the trail for a ways. See? Then he ran back onto it."

He held on to his patience. "Logically, that means Shannon is down the trail someplace. We're wasting time."

Miranda's face turned red. "Listen, Blaylock. No one wants to find my sister faster than I do. But if we go barreling down the trail and wipe out Poker's tracks, how are we going to find where Shannon fell? She doesn't always stick to the bridle path."

He hated to admit she was right. Hated to admit that she could still rattle him. "We can ride off to one side, then. If we don't find her in a reasonable distance, we backtrack."

"Fine." She cued her gelding into a lope.

"Miranda."

She shot a sideways look at him.

"Sorry."

Her blue eyes burned into his. "Just help me find my sister."

Minutes later, they located where Poker's tracks veered off into a meadow. A trail of trampled grass clearly showed where he'd traveled, and from the looks of things, he'd been running hard. He'd come back in the same manner, his beaten-down path through the knee-deep grass crisscrossing his original route.

Without hesitation, Miranda loped to the far side of the meadow, then pulled up to study the ground again.

"She stopped here," she said when Lucas caught up with her. "Shannon! Where are you?" The mountains echoed her words, and a pair of blackbirds flew up from a nearby pine, squawking in protest. Scattered rock and boulders, pale gray, brown and white, dotted the landscape.

Miranda leaped from the saddle. Jaw clenched, she examined the surface of one of the rocks, some five feet in diameter. Lucas could see the blood from where he sat. "She was right here," Miranda said, swallowing visibly. "So where is she now?"

He sat his horse, studying the surrounding mountains. "Her horse have any claw marks on it that I missed?"

"Not that I saw—but there was blood on the saddle."

A cougar could have knocked Shannon from the back of her horse. But it seemed Poker would be clawed if that were the case. And if a mountain lion had dragged her off, there would be signs of that. His stomach churned at the thought.

He reached for the radio clipped to his belt, but all he got was static. "Damn battery's weak." He looked down at Miranda. "Come on. We'll ride back to meet Garrett. Organize a search party."

She shook her head and swung back onto her horse. "I'm going to keep looking."

"Don't be stubborn." Lucas gestured around them. "You've got rock face going off in twenty different directions. Shannon could be anywhere. You'll never find her trail going it alone."

Miranda raised her chin. "She's my sister. She's hurt and we're wasting time." With that, she spun the gelding around and headed up a trail fit only for mountain goats.

Lucas shook his head. He started to call to her to come back as the gray shifted beneath him, then decided not to waste his breath. "Danged stubborn, fool woman."

Still, he couldn't help but admire her strength and courage. Just like her mom's. He wished his own mother would've had some.

Maybe then she'd still be alive.

CHAPTER TWO

MIRANDA VOWED TO RIDE until hell froze over, if that's what it took to find Shannon. And Lucas Blaylock could eat skunk and die if he didn't approve. He'd been a thorn in her side since she was fourteen. And at twenty, he'd broken her heart and humiliated her in front of all her friends and family.

She should've listened to her mother.

With a younger brother who always managed to find trouble, and an alcoholic father who liked to use his fists, Lucas had fought his way through life with a go-to-hell attitude. He'd been three years older than her and twice as wild.

When Miranda was a teenager, her mother's biggest fear had been that her daughters would fall for one of the Blaylock boys. Miranda had fallen, all right. Head over heels crazy for Lucas Blaylock, with his sandy hair—worn a bit too long—and icy blue eyes. She'd defied her mom and went after him.

He'd gradually outgrown his bad habits, and hadn't turned out anything like his jailbird father or his wife-beating brother. Instead, he'd become a lawman.

Yet his white-knight syndrome hadn't stopped him from leaving Miranda.

She halted Sundae on a rocky plateau. Around her, the mountains rose abruptly, too steep for a horse to climb. But not for a person. Had Shannon hiked out of here for some reason? Logic told Miranda her sister couldn't climb these rocks injured. But what if she had a head wound that had left her disoriented? She could've wandered off and gotten lost.

"Shannon!" Miranda gathered her reins as Sundae fidgeted, eager to go. Had Shannon ridden to higher ground and fallen off her horse? Was she lying unconscious in a ravine? Refusing to admit Lucas had a point—that it would be smarter to wait for search and rescue—Shannon turned the gelding and headed back down the trail. Halfway to the bottom, she veered off in a different direction, looking for tracks, blood, any sign that Shannon or Poker had been here....

She checked everywhere she could think of that she and Shannon had ridden in the past, and explored a few places they hadn't. Frustrated, she headed back down into the valley and stopped to let Sundae drink at a stream. She looked up at the sound of hoofbeats.

Paige. Her mother pulled her sorrel mare to a halt. "No luck?" The expression on her wan face was as hopeless as a lost child's.

Miranda shook her head. "Did Lucas get a search party organized?"

"Yes. He called in every available deputy and volunteer he could find. Word's spreading fast. A bunch of our neighbors have shown up to help—Tori's there." Miranda's best friend since third grade. "They're forming a search grid. You want to ride back with me and join them?"

Miranda sighed. "Yeah. I've looked everywhere I can think of."

They rode in silence for a while.

"How could she just vanish?" Paige's choked voice hit Miranda hard. "If it wasn't a mountain lion…" She let out a sob, and Miranda knew where her mind had gone.

To a night months ago, when Shannon might've become a victim of the man she'd helped send to jail. A night in the dark parking lot of the Silver Spur, where she had witnessed the abduction of Jo Ella Jamison.

Abducted by a guy Shannon had danced with in the bar that night.

"Mom. Don't think that way." Miranda inched Sundae up beside her mother's horse. "We're going to find her."

But deep down inside, she was just as scared as Paige.

"I DON'T WANT TO LEAVE you alone." Miranda slumped in a chair in the living room, every inch of her body aching.

"Me, neither." Tori, with her blazing red hair and flashy Western clothes, had never looked more serious.

"You girls are tired," Paige said. "Go on home. I'll be fine."

But she didn't look fine. They'd searched until dark closed in around them, and still hadn't found a sign of Shannon. Garrett had spotted a set of cougar tracks not far from the fork in the trail. He'd lost them when they reached rocky ground, but he'd seen no sign of human tracks, blood or anything else that would indicate the mountain lion had attacked Shannon.

Still, there was easily more than one cougar out there, as well as the occasional wolf that drifted down from Canada or up from Yellowstone National Park. No matter where Shannon was, it couldn't be good.

Lucas had questioned them until Miranda thought her head would explode. Paige had to feel the same way.

"I'll go feed, then come back."

"I'm off tonight," Tori said. She worked two jobs—waitressing at the Silver Spur and at the truck stop a few miles out of town. "I can stay, too."

Before Paige could protest, there was a knock at the back door. "Sit. I'll get it." Miranda went to the kitchen and flicked on the porch light.

"Miranda." Fae Lambert, Tori's aunt and co-owner of the truck stop, stood on the other side of the screen, one hand at her ample breast. Her black hair, coaxed with hairspray into a semitamed mane, didn't move an inch as she shook her head. "Honey, I'm so sorry to hear about Shannon. Is there any word?"

"Not yet. Come on in." Miranda held the door open, and Fae ambled inside, a plastic-wrapped pecan pie balanced on one hand. With the other she continued to clutch her brightly colored Western shirt. "I thought I'd check on you and your momma. See if there's anything Mae and I can do to help. We'll post flyers at the diner if you want."

The twin sisters had run the Truck Inn for as long as Miranda could remember. In their midfifties now, neither had ever married, but they'd raised Tori from birth when her own mother couldn't. Shirley Lambert had been diagnosed with breast cancer shortly after she found out she was pregnant. She'd refused treatment, not wanting to jeopardize her baby.

She'd died when Tori was six months old.

"That would be great," Miranda said. "Here, let me take that."

Fae handed over the pie. "We thought you might need a little something to keep you going. And by the way, Mae says to tell you to stop by the diner on your way home. She's got a fresh pot of coffee on and a big ol' kettle of hunter's stew. You'll need it if you keep riding these hills all day and night."

With that, she swept into the living room, where she enveloped Miranda's mom in a hug. "Paige, honey, I'm so sorry. I wish there was something more I could do."

Paige returned the embrace. "Thank you. I'm about

half out of my mind." She gestured toward a recliner, then sat down herself. "Can you stay awhile?"

"I sure can. As long as you need me to."

"Mom—"

"Don't 'Mom' me," Paige said. "See, I told you I'll be fine. Go home, girls." She looked from one to the other. "Get some rest. Fae's here with me now." But her voice sounded nasal, and moisture rimmed her eyes.

Miranda sank onto the couch beside her and rubbed her mother's back. "Don't worry. We're going to find her."

"Of course we will." Paige shooed her away. "Get some of Mae's stew and take care of your animals."

"All right. But if you change your mind, call me."

"I will."

"Thanks, Fae."

"You betcha. I'll take good care of your momma."

Outside, Miranda climbed into her truck. "You coming with me?" she asked Tori.

Her friend shook her head. "Lord knows I spend enough time at that place as it is. Unless you need me to," she quickly added. "Of course I'll come." She started to walk around the front of the truck.

"No, it's okay, Tori." Miranda started the truck and glanced at the dashboard clock. Ten-fifteen. "I'm just going to grab something quick, then head home. I'll call you tomorrow."

"All right then." Tori leaned on the truck's half-open door. "Try not to worry. We *will* find Shannon."

"I know." But as Miranda drove to town, she continued to worry. She wasn't particularly hungry, and she knew her animals waiting at home were, but right now she felt as though she could barely drag her tired body through chores. A cup of Mae's famous stand-a-spoon-in-it coffee sounded pretty good. Maybe a jolt of caffeine would revive her. Miranda doubted she'd sleep tonight, anyway, worn-out or not. The thought of Shannon hurt and scared out there—God knew where—wouldn't leave.

The flashing neon lights of the Truck Inn came into view, casting a green-and-pink glow over the asphalt. Miranda parked and walked past the motel and gas station to the diner. Mae stood behind the counter, a clone of her twin, save for her bright red hair. She wore a frilly, plus-size Western blouse and black jeans that were a tad snug. She waved Miranda over the minute she stepped through the door.

"Miranda, honey, I've got a bowl of stew with your name on it." Before she could protest, Mae set a plain white bowl, heaped full, on the counter, then poured a steaming mug of coffee. "This will get you goin'. No mocha lattes here." She winked. Whipping out a napkin and silverware with a practiced ease acquired from waiting on hungry truck drivers for decades, Mae urged her to sit down. "Any word on Shannon?"

"Not yet." Miranda blew on the coffee, then took a cautious sip. The strong brew nearly made her hair stand on end. *Cowboy coffee.* She set it down and added sugar. "The search party rode till dark. We're going to pick up again at daylight."

"Tori called earlier. Said there was folks on horses, ATVs and on foot." Mae shook her head. "You know, my fanny might be a tad too wide to ride, but I can still manage a hike. You let me know if you need an extra pair of eyes and I'll be there with bells on."

Miranda gave her a tired smile. "Thanks, Mae. I sure appreciate it."

A few customers sidled over and began to question Miranda about what had happened. She talked until she thought her brain would explode. The fact that her sister's disappearance had become a source of gossip made her sick.

Leaving her stew half-finished, she threw some money on the counter. "I've gotta get home and feed. Thanks for the stew and coffee, Mae."

"Anytime, sweetie. Anytime." Mae swept the bowl out of sight and wiped the counter with an oversize damp cloth.

Outside, Miranda pointed her Chevy down the road. Her head felt woozy from lack of sleep. Even the coffee hadn't helped as much as she'd hoped. Rolling down her window for a blast of cool night air, she focused on the drive.

She'd barely started down the highway that led to the county road turnoff for her ranch when she spotted flashing lights in her rearview mirror. Heart pounding, Miranda pulled over. *Shannon. They'd found Shannon.*

She was out of the truck before the familiar, dark green Blazer had even come to a complete stop behind her. Lucas slid from the SUV, scowling.

"You're supposed to stay in your vehicle when an officer of the law pulls you over."

"Did you find her?"

"What? No." His features softened. "That's not why I stopped you."

"So, what—I have a taillight out? I was going fifty in a forty-five?" She folded her arms. "Lucas, I'm tired. Just write me a ticket for whatever I've done and I'll be on my way."

"Are you always such delightful company?" He glared at her from beneath the brim of his hat; his face backlit by his headlights.

She still found him far too attractive.

"Are you always on duty? For crying out loud, I thought you'd be home sleeping by now."

"I could say the same of you, which, by the way, is why I pulled you over. You were weaving across the dotted line."

"I wasn't." Miranda frowned. "Was I?"

"You're dog-tired, with no business being behind the wheel. You could kill yourself—or someone else."

She felt stupid. "You're right. I'm sorry."

Lucas gestured, official-like. "Pull your truck over on that wide spot there and park it. You can get it in the morning after you've had some sleep."

She let her jaw drop. "And how do you expect me

to get home?" He simply raised his brows. "Oh, no. I'm not riding with you."

"Yes, you are."

"Lucas, I'm fine. I'm less than three miles from home."

"Move your truck. Now." He spun on his heel.

Cursing under her breath, even though she knew he was right, Miranda stomped over to the Chevy and moved it onto the pull off beside the highway. After locking the doors, she got into the passenger seat of the Blazer, refusing to look at Lucas. It was bad enough she'd had to be around him the better part of the day. But if he helped find Shannon…that was all that mattered.

He drove in silence for a few minutes, with only the crackle of his police radio as background noise.

"Don't you ever sleep?" she finally asked.

"On occasion."

"So you can drive tired, but I can't?"

He shot her a sideways look. "I'm used to long hours. And your mom's already beside herself with worry. She doesn't need me showing up on her doorstep telling her I scraped you out of a ditch." He turned off onto the county road.

Miranda faced straight ahead, blinking against the tired, gritty feeling behind her eyes. *Shannon. Where are you?*

Miranda's Australian shepherds, Tuck and Smudge, trotted down the driveway, barking as Lucas pulled beneath the arched entrance to her ranch. The sign, hanging from it by sturdy chains, creaked in the wind. Bush Creek Ranch—Barrel Racing Clinic. Horses Broke and Trained. Lessons Available.

Surrounded by mountains, thick timber and brush, her one hundred acres was a haven, the seclusion more than welcome after such a stressful day.

"Thanks for the ride," Miranda said grudgingly. She'd opened the door and gotten out when, to her annoyance, Lucas turned off the engine and did the same. She slammed the passenger door. "What are you doing?"

"Helping you feed. I'm officially off duty in two minutes."

"I don't need help, thanks."

"Don't be so damn stubborn. It's late. Listen to them." He nodded toward the barn and surrounding corrals. Horses whinnied and nickered, impatient at having missed their evening meal. "Two can feed faster than one."

She didn't want him here. Didn't want to have a thing to do with the man who'd left her in a church and a white dress. But she needed him to help find Shannon.

Clamping her lips together, Miranda led the way to the barn. She pulled bales from the haystack and cut the twine, not saying a word. She knew she was behaving ungratefully—that she should thank Lucas for lending a hand, despite their personal grudges.

It was as she threw hay to the pretty red roan in the

last stall that Miranda's emotions got the best of her. She bit her lip—hard—and blinked back tears. She'd been training the roan as a barrel horse. For Shannon.

"Miranda?" Lucas laid a hand on her shoulder.

She shrugged away as though she'd been burned. "I'm fine. Just stretching my neck." She moved her head back and forth, massaging her pinched muscles.

"Let me." She tried to knock them aside, but his hands found their way to either edge of her collarbone, and he worked his strong thumbs and fingers up and down her shoulders, her neck, getting rid of the kinks.

She closed her eyes, fighting her misgivings. The past was the past. Shannon was missing and possibly in grave danger, out in the wilderness alone—or worse. Up until that very minute, Miranda had wanted to pretend her sister was all right. That she'd merely taken a spill from her horse, whacked her head and gotten disoriented. That she'd show up any minute now on their mother's doorstep, hurt but okay. She would laughingly explain what had happened. *Lost my bearings. Got turned around in the trees and the dark.*

But Shannon knew the woods and mountains like her own backyard. They *were* her backyard. One she and Miranda had grown up in, riding with their mom. Taking groups out with Paige from the time they were old enough to sit a horse.

Miranda stepped away from Lucas again and dropped onto a bale of hay. "I can't stop thinking about Jo Ella." She was just twenty-one. Shannon was older, probably stronger. Could she fight off an attacker? Was that where the blood had come from?

"Miranda, Lonnie Masterson is in jail. He can't hurt Shannon."

"He's not the only kook out there, you know. Bad things happen in small towns, too."

Lucas let out a tired sigh. "Try not to worry," he said. "We're going to find her."

Miranda bit her lips again, nodding. "Yeah."

But would it be too late?

CHAPTER THREE

LUCAS FOLLOWED MIRANDA to the house, accepting her offer of a Coke to go. He needed caffeine. But when he walked into the living room, he collapsed, every tired bone in his body aching. He perched on the end of the black leather couch. Just for a minute. The gray-and-blue throw pillows behind him, embroidered with horses, felt mighty inviting.

Miranda narrowed her eyes when she handed him his Coke a moment later, but said nothing. Instead, she slipped off her boots and sat at the opposite end of the couch, tucking her feet beneath her. "So, what's the plan for tomorrow?"

"We'll get the search team out again...more volunteers. Kyle Miller's living in Bozeman now, working with search and rescue." Miranda had dated Kyle, back when they were kids. "He's got a tracking dog. I spoke to Kyle earlier, and he's going to bring the dog over. We'll see if he can pick up Shannon's trail."

Hope lit Miranda's eyes. "Good. I still can't believe this is happening." She pulled the band from her ponytail and raked a hand through her long, dark hair. Lucas recalled how tense her muscles had felt when he'd rubbed her neck and shoulders. He wished she'd let him comfort her.

Quiet claimed the room as Miranda sat lost in thought. Lucas let his own mind drift, mapping out the search procedure for tomorrow. They had to find Shannon. He wouldn't rest until they did.

He wasn't even aware that he'd dozed off until he awoke with a jerk. Disoriented for a moment, Lucas wondered where he was. Finding Miranda snuggled against him answered that question. She slept fitfully, her forehead creased. Her hair tumbled in disarray around her shoulders. It looked as if she'd fallen asleep, then inched her way prone, her knees now tucked close to her chest as she lay curled against him. She murmured something in her sleep.

Unable to resist, he reached down and caressed her face. If only things could be different...

She sighed, and the tense lines relaxed as he stroked her. The rough-and-tumble cowgirl—not afraid to ride the wildest horse or even a bull in her high school days—felt soft and feminine beneath his hand, her body warm. He hated to wake her, and wished he could stretch out beside her and wrap her in his arms.

"Miranda," he said softly. She came instantly awake. Her eyes shot open, and widened when she saw him. She sat up.

"I guess I *was* tired. What are you still doing here?"

"I dozed off, too."

"What time is it?" She covered a yawn and turned to look at the clock on the wall. "*Five?* Crud. I need to shower." She rose quickly. "The search party's going to meet at six?"

He nodded.

"Cripes! I forgot I don't have my truck." She glared at him, dispelling all fantasies he'd harbored a moment ago.

"I'll run you to get it after your shower. Meanwhile, I'll head home and take one myself. Need any help with your morning chores?"

"No, thanks. You've done enough."

"Okay. See you in a bit."

When he walked outside, the dogs circled and nipped at his heels. "Hey, knock it off!" He kept an eye on them over his shoulder as they followed him to the Blazer, barking once he was inside.

It was as though they were telling him what he already knew. He didn't belong here with Miranda.

And he'd do well to remember that.

MIRANDA TRAILERED RANGER, her black gelding, over to the stables. Searchers were already gathering, along with a couple of reporters from the local press. Lucas had brought his own horse, too, a stocky buckskin. Within a short time, Miranda had Ranger saddled, ready to ride. A silver SUV pulled up by the barn, and a tall man wearing a ball cap—Kyle Miller—unloaded a black German shepherd from the back. Miranda had expected a bloodhound. Then again, she'd seen other breeds used for tracking. She watched as Kyle spoke to Lucas, then the two came toward her and Paige.

"Kyle," Miranda said. "I haven't seen you since ninth grade. I almost didn't recognize you with the mustache and all." He sported a neatly trimmed, goatee-style beard.

"I've been hearing that ever since I moved back to Montana," he said, his dark eyes taking her in.

"Thank you for coming, Kyle," Paige said.

"I'm happy to help. I'm just sorry I couldn't get out here yesterday. We were conducting a search for a lost child over in Blue Ridge Park. Found him, safe and sound." Kyle beamed proudly at the big shepherd. "If your daughter is out there, Blackhawk will find her."

"I sure hope so."

"Do you still ride?" Miranda asked. "Will your dog follow a horse?"

"I ride, and Blackhawk will stick with me. But to work the scent, I need to be on foot."

"That's fine, but it's a ways out to the place where Shannon's trail disappeared. It'll be faster to get there on horseback."

"That'll do. We can work the trail from there. I'll need an item of Shannon's clothing, preferably something she's recently worn."

"I already have it," Paige said. She handed over a paper bag. "It's one of her T-shirts."

"Perfect."

"Okay," Miranda said. "Let's go."

Kyle mounted up on one of the dude horses, and the four of them headed out the east fork, while Garrett and Deputy Mac Frazier stayed behind to supervise a search grid. In spite of the mild early morning temperature, Miranda shivered as they neared the rock where they'd found Shannon's blood.

Kyle climbed off his horse and traded Blackhawk's collar for a leash and harness. The dog grew excited. It was time to work. Kyle took Shannon's T-shirt and let the animal sniff it, giving him encouragement and the command "Go find."

Miranda watched, fascinated, as the shepherd sniffed the rock, then lowered his head to investigate the patch of blood, which had dried to a dark brown. He circled and immediately picked up a scent. He set off, Kyle clutching the long lead, the pair climbing the steep hillside in a direction Miranda hadn't taken yesterday. One too steep for the horses to go.

Dismounting, she handed her reins to her mother. "Will you wait here? Hold Ranger for me, Mom?"

Paige nodded. Her anxious expression told Miranda she was afraid of what the dog might find. Which was precisely why Miranda wanted to go without her.

Lucas left the buckskin's reins dangling. "He

won't go anywhere as long as the other horses stay put, Paige. You'll be all right by yourself?" He gave Miranda a pointed look.

"I'm going," she reiterated.

"All right."

"It's okay—go," Paige said. But she looked scared, and the bags beneath her eyes told Miranda she'd cried herself to sleep last night. Paige rarely cried.

Determined to find her sister, one way or another, Miranda climbed.

"We need to keep back out of Kyle's way," Lucas said.

"I understand."

"Now you can see what I was trying to tell you yesterday," he said. "That Shannon could've gone in any direction."

Miranda's face warmed with resentment. "I realize that. But I told you. I had to try to find her."

"We will."

They continued to climb, the going impossibly steep for a long stretch, the ground too hard-packed and rocky to see footprints. Then Blackhawk and Kyle angled off on a game trail that took a less perilous route. They wound through brush and rock, steadily climbing before dropping down again toward a gully.

"I hope this dog knows what he's doing," Miranda muttered. Below, Paige and the horses had become dots in the distance, then disappeared.

"He's the best," Lucas said. He paused to catch his breath, forcing Miranda to halt as well, then continued on.

Twenty minutes later, they heard the sound of moving water. Up ahead a wide stream pooled into a small lake. If Shannon had somehow managed to cross the water, would Blackhawk be able to pick up her trail on the other side? The stream definitely wasn't small enough to jump. So how *would* Shannon have crossed it, if she were injured?

Unless she hadn't been on her own.

Miranda swallowed hard, and for a moment, she couldn't breathe. Briefly, she squeezed her eyes shut and forced herself to calm down.

The brush grew thicker, and Blackhawk and Kyle disappeared into the midst of it. Lucas hurried to catch up, Miranda on his heels. A staccato bark, followed by a triumphant shout, reached their ears as they burst from the cover and came out on the stream bank.

Kyle stooped to praise and pet his dog, rewarding him with a ball on a rope. "Good boy, Blackhawk! Atta boy."

"What?" Miranda asked. "What did he find?" She didn't see anything on the rocky creek bed. Then Kyle pointed out a bit of color at the edge of the water.

"There," he said.

She gasped. A faded, teal-blue scrunchie. The one Shannon had used to pull her hair into a ponytail yesterday before she rode away.

"That's Shannon's," Miranda said, bending to reach for it.

"Don't touch it," Lucas said sharply. From his shirt pocket, he took out a digital camera and began to snap pictures, then extracted a plastic evidence bag from his denim jacket. Using a pen, he lifted the scrunchie and put it in the bag.

"She was here," Miranda said unnecessarily.

"She must've crossed the water," Lucas said, staring at the rapidly flowing stream. "Can you pick up her trail on the other side, Kyle?"

"I can sure try." Kyle studied the area, as did Lucas and Miranda.

"We need to find a better place to cross," Lucas said. "The water's too fast here." He frowned. "Are you sure the trail stops dead right here?"

Kyle nodded. "Blackhawk would've gone on if it followed the bank."

"All right, then," Lucas said, his jaw set. "We'll just find a place to cross. But we need to mark this area." He took off his denim jacket, unloaded the pockets and tied it to a sapling near the water's edge. Then he gathered some rocks, with Miranda's and Kyle's help, and at the base of the tree made a pile that could be seen for some distance. "That ought to do." He pocketed the evidence bag. "Let's go."

The three of them set out along the creek bank, picking their way through brush and rock. It was a good while before they found a possible place to cross, where the water was shallow and enough exposed rock and gravel provided a makeshift footbridge to the other side. Blackhawk splashed on in, not seeming to mind getting wet, and Miranda studied the dog to see if he picked up anything. Had Shannon found this crossing and used it? Or had she gone through the water at another spot?

Trying not to despair at the enormity of the task ahead, Miranda watched Kyle once again take Shannon's T-shirt from the bag Paige had given him, and wave it under Blackhawk's nose. The shepherd sniffed it and then, at Kyle's instruction, began searching the ground.

They headed back the direction they'd come, keeping an eye out for the sapling Lucas had marked with his jacket. If Shannon had emerged from the stream at any point near where she'd dropped her hair tie, they ought to be able to find her trail. But though Kyle worked Blackhawk up one side and down the other, the shepherd came up empty.

"Why the hell isn't he finding her scent?" Miranda closed her eyes. "Sorry. That was uncalled for."

"Understandable," Kyle said.

"I appreciate your help," Miranda added. She knew Kyle would do anything in his power to find her sister.

He halted, frowning. "Maybe we ought to search around the lake.

"Keep your eye out for tracks," Lucas said unnecessarily as they headed downstream. But though they walked the entire perimeter of the lake, they didn't see any human footprints. And Blackhawk still picked up nothing.

After an hour, they stopped to rest.

Kyle looked as frustrated as Miranda felt. "I'm sorry, Miranda," he said. "I don't understand this. Unless your sister came out of the water at a place we haven't covered yet."

"I don't see how that could be," Lucas said, taking off his hat to wipe sweat from his brow with the back of his forearm. "We've gone about as far in both directions as a person could expect to walk."

Miranda dropped onto a fallen log, feeling more helpless than she ever had in her life. She folded her arms to keep from shaking. "She'd never wander off this far willingly. My God, she could be in the hands of a rapist…a killer." Miranda met Lucas's gaze. "I know Lonnie Masterson's in jail, but what about a copycat…?" She couldn't bring herself to say it.

Copycat killer.

Lucas wrapped one arm around her shoulders. "Hey. Calm down, Miranda. This is a positive lead. We found her hair tie, and we're going to find her."

"Positive?" She pulled away from him. "How can you say that? The only thing I'm positive about is that some maniac has kidnapped my sister." Unable to stop the tears, she angrily wiped them away. "Damn it! Why? Why Shannon? Lucas, what has happened to my sister?"

"I don't know," he said darkly. "But I'm damn sure going to find out. Let's head back to the horses."

CHAPTER FOUR

"DID YOU FIND ANYTHING, Sheriff Blaylock?"

"Mrs. Ward, is it true there were blood and claw marks on your daughter's horse?"

"Back off!" Miranda thumped her heels against Ranger's sides, plowing through the group of reporters circling her mom like a pack of wolves. Cameramen and journalists scattered.

"Hey, that's expensive equipment, lady!" A tall, skinny guy reached for his zoom lens, which had fallen in the dirt.

"And this is private property." Miranda stared him down.

"Clear out," Lucas said above the hubbub of the crowd.

Miranda had expected the press, but she'd never thought they'd come en masse. News trucks and cars from every television and radio station within a hundred-mile radius lined the ranch's driveway. Thankfully, Lucas and his deputies somehow got them all to leave.

"Chet," Paige said, "Go down and close the gate, will you please?"

"Yes, ma'am." The lanky cowboy turned his horse and trotted off.

A camera flash went off in Miranda's face just as she swung down from the saddle. She managed to get her foot out of the stirrup before stumbling into Lucas.

Where in thunder had it come from?

"I thought you were told to leave," the sheriff growled. He took a menacing step toward the reporter, his horse's reins clutched in one hand, the other fisted at his side. "Get the hell away from that tree and out of here, or so help me God I'll throw you in jail for trespassing!"

Miranda barely heard him. Spots from the camera's flash danced across her vision. It took a half minute to realize that wasn't the cause of her nauseating dizziness. It was the memory of another camera. Another newspaper reporter.

Smile now, lovebirds. That's it. Look like you're already on your honeymoon. Perfect...

The woman who wrote the local wedding and engagement column for the *Sage Bend News* had had Miranda and Lucas pose for several shots to make sure she had a good one. The photo appeared the following day on page three, Lucas looking sexy in his white hat and Western suit as he smiled for the camera; Miranda, clearly happy, in a melon-colored dress Shannon had helped her pick out. She'd felt like the luckiest woman on earth as she'd leaned into Lucas, his arm wrapped protectively—lovingly—around her waist, her hand on his as though she'd never let go....

Miranda took a deep breath, and her queasiness gradually faded. At the sound of tires crunching over gravel, she looked down the driveway to see an old, beat-up pickup truck heading their way.

"Lucas, isn't that your sister-in-law?" Paige asked.

"Yep." Lucas stood waiting beside Miranda as Dena Blaylock got out of her truck, a large box cradled in her arms.

Lucas passed his reins to Miranda and moved to help as Dena extended her offering. The sleeve of the other woman's shirt rode up an inch or so, and Miranda saw a greenish-yellow, days-old bruise on her wrist.

"Hi, Miranda," Dena said, tugging at her sleeve. "Chet let me through the gate, Paige. I hope you don't mind me dropping by. I heard about Shannon, and I wanted to help search, but my gelding's lame." She indicated what she'd brought. "I thought y'all could use some comfort food to tide you over for a couple of days, so you won't have to worry about cooking."

"That was thoughtful," Paige said, taking it from Lucas. "Thank you, Dena."

"There's a couple of casseroles, and I made some

stew…and some beans and ham hock in freezer bags. You can just thaw and heat them whenever you need to."

"What did you do to your arm, Dena?" Miranda asked, even though it was none of her business. She already knew the answer anyway. But with Shannon missing—possibly the victim of violence—her tolerance was flat zero.

Dena lowered her gaze and tugged at her sleeve again. "I sprained it. Fell off a haystack unloading some bales into the loft." She shrugged. "I've always been clumsy."

"Especially since you married my brother," Lucas said, clenching his jaw.

Dena and Clint had been married for a while… five years? Miranda thought that was about right. According to gossip, Clint had started roughing Dena up not long after their honeymoon, and had since progressed to knocking the crap out of her whenever he felt like it, which was most of the time. They had two kids, and a reputation for fighting like a couple of bobcats in a burlap bag.

Miranda was surprised they hadn't killed one another by now. She felt sorry for their children.

Dena faced her. "I just wanted to come out and tell you how sorry I am to hear about your sister."

"Thank you," Miranda said, wishing Dena would take her kids and go to a battered women's shelter.

Lucas's steely expression let Miranda know Dena

wasn't fooling him, either. "Tell Clint I'll stop by and say howdy as soon as I brush my horse down."

Dena went white. "There's no need, Lucas. You've got your hands full here."

He merely grunted—a familiar sound Miranda knew meant the subject was closed. Without further argument, Dena turned and left.

"I'll brush Cimarron." Miranda gave him a meaningful look. "You go ahead, Lucas."

"Thanks. I'll be back shortly. Paige, try not to worry. We'll find Shannon."

Paige merely nodded.

Lucas addressed the volunteers as they gathered around, telling them about finding Shannon's hair tie. "There's other ways to get to that lake and the area around it," he said. "We'll all meet back here at one-thirty—divide into groups. We'll decide which areas we should search next. We might have a dead end for now, but it's possible we can still pick up a lead."

"I'll be happy to come back," Kyle offered. "Maybe Blackhawk can find something yet."

Miranda thanked him, then watched Lucas climb into his Blazer and drive away, the empty horse trailer rattling behind him. Several other people left as well, promising to rejoin the search later.

"Me and Chet can brush those horses down for you, Miranda," Sam said, his bright blue eyes sympathetic. "Yours, too, Miss Paige. Why don't you go inside and put your feet up for a spell." Miranda appreciated the older cowboy trying to comfort her. "Thanks anyway, Sam, but I could use something to keep me busy."

"You can take Snap," Paige said, handing the mare over. "I need to get this food put away and go help with lunch." One of the neighboring ranchers had offered to feed the volunteers a hearty meal.

"I'm going to see Tori after I finish with the horses," Miranda told her, "but I won't be gone long." Tori's shift at the Silver Spur had kept her from being at the ranch today.

Paige nodded, then headed for the back door. Miranda led Ranger and Cimarron toward the barn. She cross-tied each horse in the aisle, looking over at Poker's stall. A lump swelled in her throat. The big bay gelding had settled down, and now stood contentedly munching hay from his feeder, oblivious to the fate of his owner.

"I sure wish you could talk," she murmured.

As she unsaddled and brushed Ranger, Miranda's thoughts drifted from Shannon to Lucas. She'd like to be a fly on the wall when he confronted Clint, the sorry SOB. She couldn't understand why Dena put up with the abuse he dished out.

But most of all, Miranda had never come to terms with the fact that Lucas thought he was no better than his brother or his father, which was why he'd decided not to marry her, after all.

Apples and oranges.

But nothing Miranda had said could convince him otherwise.

LUCAS DROVE FASTER THAN he should have on his way to Clint's place, especially since he hadn't taken the time to unhitch his trailer. He knew his efforts were futile, but some small part of him still hoped he could shake his brother up enough to get him to back off from abusing Dena. Lucas constantly worried for her safety. And right now, he wasn't exactly in a happy frame of mind.

He hadn't wanted to upset Miranda any more than she already was. But when she'd brought up the possibility of a copycat killer, one thing had come to mind: Lonnie Masterson himself very well could be behind Shannon's abduction. It was possible he had friends on the outside more than willing to help him make the only witness for his prosecution disappear.

The thought made Lucas insane. He and Miranda might've broken up, but he still cared about her and her sister.

He would make arrangements to go to the Cameron County jail and have a talk with Masterson as soon as he could.

Minutes later, he arrived at his brother's place. Clint's ranch—if you could call it that—consisted of a half-dozen horses and a pack of mutts. The place lay tucked into a valley, the breathtaking scenery surrounding it a stark contrast to the shabby house. But the barn—that was another story. Clint spent most of his money on his horses, and as little as possible on Dena and the kids. For the life of him, Lucas couldn't figure out why she didn't leave his sorry ass.

Maybe it was because Dena saw the man that Clint could be if he'd only try. The man Lucas caught a glimpse of once in a while, when his brother was sober.

Lucas parked near the porch steps and was immediately swarmed by a half-dozen barking dogs, pitbulls, rottweilers and a few mutts. Ignoring them, he walked around a small tricycle and up the steps. Before he could knock, Dena opened the door. Lucas heard Cody and Jason playing in the living room, their voices carrying over the sound of the TV.

"He's not here, Lucas." Dena stepped out onto the porch, letting the screen door bang shut behind her. "But everything's okay. You don't have to worry."

"No, Dena, it's not okay." He shook his head in exasperation, but spoke low enough that the boys wouldn't hear. "Don't you get tired of him using you for a punching bag?"

"That's not fair," Dena said. "Clint's good to me…most of the time."

Lucas let out an expletive. "Fair? I'll tell you what's not fair. My worthless brother marrying one of the nicest women I know." They'd all gone to Sage Bend High, Dena and Clint just a year behind Lucas. He indicated her hidden bruise. "I've put him in jail before, and if I could prove he did that to you, I'd lock him up again."

"He needs help, not jail time." Dena rubbed her wrist. "It's nothing, really. It's just the booze talkin' when he lets his anger out."

"Yeah, well, he still has no right to knock you around." *Come on,* he urged silently. *File charges against him.*

But she wouldn't.

"So, where's he at? The Silver Spur?" The local honky-tonk was a few miles out of town, a favorite watering hole for Clint.

Dena's expression told Lucas he was right. He turned to go.

"Lucas, wait." She chewed her bottom lip. "It's not so bad." Clint's a hard worker, and I…I love him."

Lucas shook his head. "Dogged if I can puzzle that one out. See you later, Dena. Call if you need me."

He clomped down the steps and nearly tripped over a gray cat lying stretched out on the bottom one. "Where'd you come from, buddy?" he asked, surprised Clint would let Dena have a cat.

The tabby blinked and let out a scratchy-sounding meow. Standing, it laced itself through his ankles and back again, then suddenly leaped to another step, batting at a small pebble. One of the dogs came over to investigate, and the tabby gave the mutt a disdainful look and swatted its muzzle before returning to play.

Laughing, Lucas got in his Blazer and turned it

around, ignoring the dogs as they chased his rig off the property.

He forced himself to breathe deeply, exhaling through his mouth. What bothered him most was that he could almost see how Dena could still love Clint, in spite of what he did to her. Lucas remembered some good times he and his brother had had before Clint let his drinking take over his life. In many ways, Lucas loved him, and wasn't willing to give up on him. Their father was serving a sentence for using his fists one time too many—one time too hard. Lucas hated to see Clint headed down a similar path.

Dena had a point. The man needed help. Yet half the time, Lucas just wanted to beat some sense into Clint. Ironically, controlling his own temper wasn't easy.

He was a lawman on the outside. But inside, he was a Blaylock. And he knew there was a fine line keeping him from being a bastard like his brother and his father.

Lucas smacked the heel of his hand against the steering wheel. Unless Dena filed charges—or someone witnessed Clint's abuse and called the law, which had happened that one time—there was nothing Lucas could do to help her. And unless Clint wanted help, no one could force him to get it.

Lucas drove to the Silver Spur. Sure enough, Clint's pickup was in the parking lot.

And so was Miranda's.

He supposed she'd come here to talk to Tori. He

hated that Miranda might have to witness an ugly scene between him and Clint, but that's the way it had to be.

Lucas stepped inside, blinking as his eyes adjusted to the dim light. There were only a handful of patrons scattered throughout the room, and Clint was one of them. At the bar, Miranda was just sitting down. Tori put what appeared to be a glass of Coke in front of her. They both waved at him, and he nodded, then made his way over to the table where Clint sat swilling longnecks with one of his buddies.

"Look what the wind blew in," Clint said. He was half-blitzed. "Whatcha' doin' here, big brother? Did you come to see me?"

Clint's pal, Shorty, snickered. "Care to join us, Sheriff?"

"I hope neither one of you is planning to drive home." Lucas fixed them with a hard stare.

"Why, no," Clint said, his eyes widening. "We're gonna call a limo to take us home in style."

Shorty guffawed, and Clint laughed with him.

In one lightning-quick move, Lucas snatched his brother by the elbow and tugged him from the chair.

"Hey!" Clint stumbled as Lucas pulled him toward a corner of the room. "That's police brutality right there," he slurred.

"You haven't seen anything yet," Lucas said sotto voce. "Sit down, *bro*." He dropped Clint into a chair, then sat next to him. "Let's get something straight. I don't like the way you're treating your wife. And it had better stop."

"Or else what?" Clint's eyes practically crossed as he tried to focus.

"You'll find out what," Lucas said. He only wished both Clint and Dena had neighbors close by. Living so far out in the country left Dena and the kids vulnerable. "I'll lock you up until you rot."

Clint leaned back in his chair and laughed. "No worries, *Lukie*. I treat Dena like a queen."

"Yeah. I saw the bruise. What about the kids, Clint? Don't you ever think of them?"

"There's nothing wrong with my kids," Clint mumbled. "I feed 'em and clothe 'em."

"Barely." Lucas leaned close to Clint's ear, trying not to breathe the alcohol fumes. "You'd better walk the line, Clint. I mean it." He stood. "Now hand over your keys."

Clint gave him a dirty look, then reluctantly fished the keys to the beat-up Dodge out of his pocket. He slapped them down on the table, and Lucas pocketed them.

"I'll leave them at your house."

"How am I supposed to get home?"

"Not my problem." Lucas spun on his heel, ignoring Clint as he began to sing, in a drunken, off-key tone, Johnny Cash's "I Walk the Line."

"Hey, Sheriff," Tori said. "What can I get you?"

"A glass of ice water would do fine." Lucas slid

onto the stool next to Miranda's. She looked worn-out. "I'm surprised to see you here. I'd have thought you'd get some rest after we all left."

She picked at the thin, plastic straw in her glass. "I don't think I could sleep if I tried. I just don't know what to do…where to look."

He put a hand on her shoulder. "Let me worry about that. My deputies and I won't rest until Shannon's home safe and sound."

"I know. It's just hard to sit still. Mom's going out of her mind. She's in her room with a migraine."

Lucas nodded his thanks to Tori as she placed a glass of water in front of him. He took a long pull, then set it back on the paper napkin she had whipped out from behind the bar.

"I'm gonna grab a sandwich and go back to my office," he said. "See if I can figure anything out from Shannon's phone records." Garrett was already working on a warrant for them, and for Shannon's computer, which Paige had gladly turned over to him. Since Shannon was the legal owner, they still needed the warrant to look through it. "Why don't you go home…. You've got some time before the search group meets up again. Maybe you could make a list of anything you might remember…if something comes to mind that you didn't think of before."

"Like what?"

"Shannon's behavior, anything strange beyond what you've already told me about her being scared to testify. Things she said or did in the past few days, places she went, people she talked to. You can come down to the station later and file an official missing person's report."

"All right." He read hope in her eyes, and was more determined than ever not to let her down.

Lucas ordered a ham and turkey sandwich, and Tori bustled off to get it from the kitchen. He stood and pulled his wallet from his back pocket to stuff a few bills into the tip jar. "If you want," he said to Miranda, "you can load your horse into my trailer with Cimarron when we head back out. Save you from pulling your own rig."

"Thanks, but I'd rather take mine."

"Suit yourself."

Tori came back with Lucas's sandwich, and he paid her with a ten, waving away the change.

"Where are you going to search next?" she asked.

"Everywhere we can." Lucas jerked his chin toward Clint's table. "Keep an eye on those two, will you?" He couldn't care less what happened to Clint right now. But it was his duty to protect innocent victims who might be out on the same roads. "If they try to drive, call me. I've got Clint's keys, but there's no telling with Shorty."

"Will do," Tori said. "He rode here with Clint, so I don't think you have to worry."

Lucas snorted. "I wouldn't put it past him to try to hot-wire that Dodge."

"I'll give them a ride if you want," Miranda offered. "If they're ready to leave when I go."

He stiffened. He didn't want his brother anywhere near her. Just having him in the same room with Miranda was bad enough. "I'd rather you didn't."

She scowled. "I'm a big girl, Lucas. I can take care of myself."

"I don't doubt that. But I also don't trust my brother."

"I get off at five," Tori said. "If they're still here, I'll drop them at Clint's." She waved away Lucas's protest. "I'm not afraid of them. Heck, I outweigh Shorty, and besides, both of them know better than to mess with me. If they did, there'd be hell to pay from Fae and Mae, and that's a lot of woman all told." She tucked one hand against her plump waist, striking a pose. "Or I could threaten to cut off their beer."

Miranda couldn't help but chuckle.

Lucas shook his head and walked out the door.

CHAPTER FIVE

MIRANDA RODE UNTIL SHE felt as if she'd drop from the saddle. The volunteers had met back at the Rocking W as planned. A few people offered to comb the ranch and surrounding area again for anything they might've missed, while the majority—including Miranda, Paige and Lucas—had trailered their horses to a spot where they could ride to the lake from a different direction, ending up in the area where Shannon's scrunchie had been found. Garrett and another deputy were meticulously going over both sides of the stream bank.

But they didn't find anything.

It was almost dark by the time Miranda hauled Ranger home to Brush Creek. She rubbed him down, fed and watered him along with the other horses, then took care of the dogs and barn cats. She should go inside and take a hot shower, then grab something to eat, she knew. But she wasn't hungry, and even though she was bone weary, the idea of lying in bed thinking about Shannon was more than she could bear.

Or thinking about Lucas.

He'd been so kind to her mother that he'd seemed to wear down Paige's resistance. Miranda reminded herself not to let her own defenses down. Yes, she was grateful to Lucas for all he was doing to find her sister, but that didn't erase what he'd done to her before.

With Tuck and Smudge following along, Miranda walked the path from the barn's rear exit and on through the gate. Not far away, a small stream ran past the trees, a natural, year-round source of water for her horses. She found the sound of water gurgling over the rocks soothing, unlike the roar of the big stream they'd ridden around all day.

She sat on the bank while the dogs drank from the clear water. This had always been her favorite spot to sit and think, or occasionally, to read. Long before she'd owned the ranch, when she and Lucas were teenagers, they used to sneak over here, slipping through the barbed wire fence to sit under the giant cottonwoods, where the water formed a pool there.

She and Lucas had made love here on more than one occasion at night, under the wide, starry Montana sky.

Miranda closed her eyes. She shouldn't come here anymore. Shouldn't torment herself like this. Her limbs felt heavy, her head cluttered with a jumble of thoughts. Lucas...Shannon...

She woke up to the sound of Smudge growling, followed quickly by warning barks from both dogs. Miranda sat up just in time to see Lucas—his police-issue flashlight in hand—dodge the Australian shepherds as they double-teamed him, nipping at his heels and his pant legs.

"Smudge! Tuck! Here!" Miranda whistled, and both dogs begrudgingly returned to her. She stood up, her mind still unclear. Was she dreaming?

"Damned dogs," Lucas said. He scowled at her. "What are you doing out here in the dark by yourself? For a minute, I thought you were dead." He let loose with another expletive. "You scared me half to death."

"And you scared the hell out of me." She put her hand up to shield her eyes. "Wanna turn that thing off?"

He did, and it took a minute for her eyes to readjust to the moonlight.

"You didn't answer my question," he said.

"This is my property," Miranda pointed out. "Why should you care where I sit?"

"You were asleep.... Anyone could've snuck up on you—like I did. Damn, woman. Isn't it enough that your sister is missing?"

She winced. "I didn't fall asleep intentionally, and besides, I've got my dogs." She smirked, even if he probably couldn't tell in the dark. "They were ready to take you on."

"What if the someone hadn't been me, but did have a gun?"

Miranda brushed grass and twigs from the seat of her pants. "What are you doing out here?"

"I thought I'd check on you on my way home." He

shifted, and she could hear the leather of his belt creak. "When I saw your house was dark, I figured you were asleep. So I thought…"

"Thought what? How'd you know I was out here?"

"I didn't." His tone told her he'd painted himself into a corner. "I guess I just wanted to come sit here by the creek for a few minutes."

"For old times' sake?" Miranda knew she sounded snarky, but it was the only defense she could come up with. He still remembered, too. It was unbearable.

"Something like that," Lucas mumbled.

"Well, you sit here as long as you want. I'm going to bed." She turned to walk away, and he grabbed her lightly by the elbow.

"Miranda, you know I never meant to hurt you."

A dry laugh escaped her lips. "Really? And yet you left me in the church, feeling like a fool."

"Why can't you understand that I did what was best?"

"Best for who, Lucas? For me? I don't think so." She jerked her elbow out of his grasp and flounced toward the house with him following.

She slammed the door in his face, so that he wouldn't see the tears that welled in her eyes.

"Come on, Miranda. Open up." He rapped on the screen, setting off the dogs again.

"Go away, Lucas!" Miranda wiped her hands across her cheeks. Everything finally caught up with her. The long day, the search for her sister and now…

"Are you crying? Miranda, I'm sorry. Please, just let me have a minute."

She took a deep breath, then opened the door, peering at him through the screen. "What?"

"Can I come in?"

"No. Lucas, go home. It's been a long day."

He sighed. "I know it has. And I'm sorry. For everything." He turned and left.

Miranda watched the taillights of his Blazer disappear down the road.

Then she climbed into the shower and let the water wash away the trail dust along with her tears.

LUCAS DIDN'T WASTE ANY time. He drove to the jail in neighboring Cameron County early the next morning and turned his gun and gun belt over to the deputy. Sheriff Runyon himself walked Lucas to the jailhouse and buzzed him through to the visitors' area. Lucas sat on one side of a Plexiglas partition as Lonnie Masterson, his hair buzzed short, was brought handcuffed into the small room on the other side.

Big and stocky, he wore an orange, short-sleeved jumpsuit that barely fit him, and tattoos lined his arms. He stared menacingly at Lucas, his black eyes piercing as he picked up the phone. Lucas did the same on his side.

"Well, Sheriff Blaylock, what brings you to my neck of the woods? Did you come to bring me some doughnuts?"

"We've got a missing woman in my county," Lucas said, ignoring the remark and cutting right to the chase. "Shannon Ward. What do you know about that?"

"Ah, Shannon Ward." Masterson smirked. "I know she's one sweet hunk of tail, and that I danced with her at the Silver Spur awhile back."

"Awhile back, as in the night you kidnapped and killed Jo Ella Jamison?"

Masterson's smirk disappeared, replaced by a scowl. "Now, Sheriff, that's not a very nice thing to accuse a man of. You know I didn't do anything to Jo Ella except take her out for a good time."

"Yeah. Your idea of a good time, maybe."

"Like I told you and Runyon, she was fine the last time I saw her." He grinned. "Fine as frog's hair."

"Yeah, and what about Shannon Ward?"

Lonnie raised his eyebrows. "What about her? I ain't seen her since I danced with her at the Silver Spur. Pretty little thing. You know, Sheriff, sometimes I wish I had taken her out for a good time that night instead of Jo Ella."

Lucas gripped the phone so tight he felt it might crack. He'd rather it was Lonnie's neck. "Maybe you wish Shannon weren't around to testify against you. Maybe you did something to make sure of it. Which one of your buddies on the outside have you been in touch with lately?"

Lonnie guffawed. "What do I look like? One of the Sopranos?" He leaned close to the Plexiglas. "You bet, Blaylock. I hired Guido to whack her." Then he leaned back in his chair and laughed.

"If I find out you had anything to do with Shannon's disappearance, you won't find your situation so amusing." With that, Lucas slammed down the phone.

If he were a drinking man, he thought as he drove back to town, he'd be turning to a quart of whiskey about now.

Instead, he'd settle for a good, stiff cup of Fae and Mae's coffee.

BY EIGHT-THIRTY, MIRANDA was at her computer, morning chores already behind her. From her desk, she pulled out a ream of colored paper, the pastels she used to create flyers advertising her barrel racing clinic and horse-breaking services. She'd have to rearrange her schedule and disappoint her clients, she thought numbly, as she fed pale pink sheets into her laser printer.

When she pulled up a picture of Shannon on her desktop, a lump in her throat threatened to choke her. It was a close-up shot of Shannon and Poker, standing near Paige's barn. Miranda used her software program to zoom in on her sister, then cropped the photo so that her face was clearly seen. Then she ran off several dozen copies and drove to town. She'd arranged to meet her mom and Tori at the Truck Inn.

When she got there, the two were sitting at the counter nursing cups of coffee. Booths and tables alike were full to near capacity with hungry truck drivers and local customers. Behind the counter, Fae and Mae moved with the practice of years spent at a job they enjoyed, balancing impossible numbers of platters and calling out orders to the cook. The sound of a sizzling grill drifted from the cutout divider between the kitchen and the dining room. But the smells of waffles and bacon, which would ordinarily tempt Miranda, barely registered as she sat beside her mother on one of the tall, ladder-back stools.

"Morning, honey," Mae said, plunking a white ceramic mug on the counter in front of Miranda. Hot, black coffee swirled into it, steam rising. "What can I get for you?"

"Coffee's fine," Miranda said. She laid the flyers on the counter.

"Now, you're going to need more than coffee if you're going to keep up your strength," Mae scolded. "Just ask your momma. I'll have Zane whip up some eggs and hash browns for you. It'll only take a minute." She bustled away.

"Are you all right, Mom?" Miranda eyeballed Paige's plate, which contained the better part of a waffle, the maple syrup congealed around it. "You need to eat, too."

"That's what I told her," Tori said. Her own plate had the leavings of biscuits and gravy. She pushed it away. "Guess I'm not all that hungry, either."

Paige shoved a hand through her black hair. It

looked as if she'd barely bothered to comb it. "I can't eat." She reached for one of the flyers. "You did a good job on these. I sure hope they help bring Shannon home. I saw Garrett a few minutes ago, and he said dispatch was getting quite a few calls already, but none of them have panned out."

"What kind of calls?" Miranda asked.

"Well, one guy claimed he'd seen Shannon walking with Jesus on a lake in Minnesota." She let out a snort. "Does that tell you what sort of tips they're getting?"

"Maybe so, but one of them will pay off eventually. You'll see." Miranda spoke with a confidence she didn't really feel.

"I'll put up some flyers in the windows," Mae said, as she passed by on her way to the kitchen.

"Leave us a stack of them, honey," Fae added. "We'll give them to some of the truckers running regular routes through the area. Maybe they can hang them up here and there—just in case."

"Thanks," Miranda said, dividing the flyers.

"Good morning, ladies."

Miranda turned to see Kyle standing at her elbow. He wore faded jeans and a T-shirt, his brown hair mostly hidden beneath his ball cap.

"Hi, Kyle. How's Blackhawk?"

"Raring to go, as usual. Have you got plans for continuing the search today?"

Miranda nodded. "I think everyone's pretty much

going to keep combing the areas we've partially covered." She indicated Paige and Tori. "We're going to post some flyers around town, then head out and look some more."

"Great. I can take Blackhawk out again."

"The police are directing the search and rescue," Paige said. "I'm sure they'll be thrilled to see you again…. I just want my daughter to come home."

Kyle nodded. "We'll do our best to see that happens as soon as possible." He sat at a vacant stool beside Miranda and ordered breakfast.

Miranda picked at the plate of eggs, hash browns and toast Mae set in front of her moments later. She tried to eat it, knowing Mae was right. Already, her mother appeared worn-out. Miranda wondered if she looked as tired.

But her adrenaline surged when she thought of Shannon. She forked another bite of potatoes into her mouth. The bell on the door over the café rang as customers came in and out, a sound so familiar Miranda had blocked it out. Until she caught sight of Lucas in her peripheral vision.

The food in her stomach turned sour.

"Good morning. Looks like you're all ready to get down to business." He glanced at the flyers, then Kyle.

Miranda could've sworn she saw something light in his eyes for a quick minute, something resembling jealousy. Her imagination must be playing tricks on her.

"Tell that to my aching body," Paige replied. "I thought I was used to riding long hours, until now."

"I hear you," Tori said. "I think I'm starting to walk like Festus in *Gunsmoke*."

"Well, it'll feel better once it quits hurtin'," Lucas quipped. "Kyle, don't you have a little boy to take care of? Your son—"

"Nathan." Kyle beamed. "He's with his mother this week... We're divorced," he added to Miranda.

Lucas frowned, and this time Miranda knew she wasn't imagining things.

What in the world was he doing? She glared, but Lucas merely leaned one hand on the back of her chair.

"You coming down to fill out that report?"

"As soon as I put up the flyers," she said.

"Garrett and Frank are going door-to-door, questioning as many people around and outside of town as they can. The flyers will help. Bring some with you." He tipped his hat at Paige. "Take care."

Miranda didn't even realize she'd been holding her breath until Lucas took his hand off her chair, where he'd rested it against her...probably unintentionally. Yet she'd had to fight the urge to inch forward to the edge of her seat.

She hated that he still got to her.

She waited until she was sure Lucas was gone before standing. "Are you sure you're up to helping us hang these, Mom?" she asked as she slipped a ten onto the counter.

"As much as you are," Paige retorted. But she softened her words by patting Miranda's arm. "Don't worry about me, sweetie. I'm okay. We'll get through this together, just like always." She gave her a squeeze.

"I know." Miranda managed a half smile. "You ready, Tori?"

"And willing." Her friend took a final sip of coffee before setting down her mug. "See you later, Aunt Mae. Bye, Aunt Fae." She waved.

Outside, they hopped into Miranda's truck and drove into downtown Sage Bend, which was really only a few blocks long. Miranda parked and divided up the flyers. "Shoot! I forgot the Scotch tape."

"Got it." Tori pulled a roll from her pocket.

"I brought extra," Paige said, handing some over to Miranda. "See you girls in a bit." She started down the street.

"She's a trooper," Tori said. "She'll be all right, Miranda."

"I hope so. I've never seen her look so worried or so tired."

Tori's expression softened. "I know." She bit her lip. "Let's make sure she takes it easy this afternoon."

"Right." Miranda halved the remaining flyers. "We'd both have to sit on her, and even then we'd have a battle on our hands."

The two split up, going into every place of business that was open. Miranda hadn't thought about the fact that it was Sunday, and many of the shops on

Main Street were closed. She glanced up at the sky, noting thunderheads in the distance. Still, she taped flyers on the outside of the closed retailers, knowing the owners wouldn't mind. She could always make more flyers if these got wet.

A short while later she dropped her mom and Tori back at the Truck Inn—Tori to go to work and Paige to drive her truck home.

"So, you're going to the sheriff's office?" Paige asked, leaning on the open passenger door of Miranda's pickup.

For a brief moment, Miranda wanted to ask her mother to go in her place. She knew Paige sensed her uneasiness around Lucas.

It didn't matter.

"Yeah. I'll meet you back at the ranch in a while."

Paige nodded and closed the door. But when Miranda pulled into the parking lot of the county building, her breakfast threatened to make a second appearance.

After all these years of pushing thoughts of him aside, of avoiding him at every turn, she now had to lean on him.

The man she hated every bit as much as she'd once loved him.

As HE WAITED FOR MIRANDA, Lucas used his time to go over Shannon's cell phone records. He'd had to wait the required forty-eight hours to count her as officially missing, and even though he'd gotten the cart before the horse, not having the missing person's report in hand quite yet, he'd felt compelled to carry on with his search, anyway. Everyone knew Shannon wouldn't be gone if something hadn't happened to her.

He still didn't trust Lonnie Masterson, and the thought that he would be the one to have to bring any bad news to Miranda and her mother had kept him awake the past two nights. He might have left Miranda at the altar, but he never did manage to get her out of his head.

What an idiot he'd been last night. He had no idea why he'd gone to the stream. Maybe instinct had led him to Miranda. They'd been so close, they used to practically read each other's minds. Until he'd blown it.

And now, Kyle Miller was lurking about. A single father, probably just looking to give little Nathan a new stepmommy. Lucas set his jaw. He knew he was being an ass—that he owed a lot to Kyle for searching with his dog. Yet when he'd seen the guy sitting right there next to Miranda at the truck stop…

The sound of her footsteps drew his attention. She halted in his doorway, looking determined but tired. Her dark hair was pulled back in a ponytail beneath a black cowboy hat, and the blue in the shirt she wore brought out the color of her eyes.

"Come on in," he said gruffly, furious that he

should notice such things. He barely glanced at her when she took the chair on the other side of his desk.

She laid some flyers down. "I'll let you hang these on your bulletin board...wherever else you want. Tori, Mom and I practically wallpapered the town with them. I thought I'd put some up in your windows, too."

"That's fine." From his desk, Lucas picked up the copy of Shannon's cell phone records he'd obtained that morning. "You want to take a look at this and tell me if you recognize any of the numbers on it?"

"The ranch number is on here...Mom's. Mine, too, and my cell." Miranda stared at the piece of paper. "Other than those, I don't recognize any of them."

"All right, then. We'll dial the rest and see what we get." He slid the missing person's form in front of her with a pen across it. "The DA's having a hissy fit over Shannon's disappearance, her being his key witness in Masterson's trial. He's calling in the state police."

"We can use all the help we can get," Miranda said. "But as far as the DA, it's not his trial I'm worried about. I need to know where my sister is. I need to find her safe and sound." Her blue eyes darkened. "That's all that matters to me."

"I understand. Did you make a list of anything you might've forgotten before?"

She shook her head. "I honestly can't think of anything. I mean, Shannon's been uptight, worried about the trial and all. But nothing specific comes to mind."

He nodded. "Is Kyle going to bring his dog out to the ranch again?"

Miranda paused, pen in hand. "What is up with your attitude?"

He felt his face heat. "What attitude?"

"You know damn good and well what I'm talking about. You were rude to Kyle at the truck stop."

"I was not."

She merely raised an eyebrow.

"Okay, so maybe I wasn't as grateful as I should've been to the guy. I guess I'm tired." He leaned back in his chair. "Is he coming back out to the ranch or not?"

"I think so. He's been working Blackhawk in various areas, from what I understand."

"I know. He's been a big help," Lucas said.

Hell, he'd call up Brad Pitt, Johnny Depp *and* Orlando Bloom if he thought it would help take the sadness from Miranda's eyes.

He started to give her his word that he'd find Shannon, until he remembered his word didn't mean much to her anymore.

MIRANDA HAD JUST FINISHED taping a couple of flyers to either side of the sheriff's office windows when she looked across the street and spotted Vance Porter and his yellow dog. With a reputation as Sage Bend's proverbially reclusive mountain man, Vance came to town only when he had to. As Miranda watched, the fiftysomething man snatched a flyer off the window of the antique shop, glanced around, then slipped the paper inside his shirt.

"Hey!" Miranda shouted as she pushed through the glass doors and ran across the street. "What do you think you're doing?"

He turned to her, narrowing his dark brown eyes, his lips dotted with flecks of chewing tobacco. Beneath his gray cowboy hat, his salt-and-pepper hair was cropped military style, his almond-brown face creased into an embarrassed smile.

The yellow Labrador barked at Miranda, then wagged its tail.

"Can't a feller look in a shop window without being accosted?" Vance spat into the gutter.

"You took my flyer," Miranda accused, indicating the chambray shirt he wore over a T-shirt. "Put it back."

"I didn't see your name on it," Vance said, drawing back like a spiteful child.

"No, but it has my sister's photo on it, and she's been missing since Friday. You wouldn't happen to know anything about that, would you?" She folded her arms and stared him down.

"Listen here, missy. I've knowed your momma since before you was even born. Don't you go gettin' sassy with me."

"Cough it up," Miranda said, holding out her hand.

Vance ground his teeth, then reached inside his

shirt and grudgingly produced the rolled-up flyer. "You've got plenty of them," he grumbled.

Miranda snatched the paper from him, smoothed the wrinkles out against the window glass, then applied a fresh piece of tape before rounding on Vance again. "Why did you take it?"

"I didn't mean no harm," the man said nervously, as Lucas jogged across the street. "Really, I didn't."

"What's going on?" Lucas demanded.

"He took one of my flyers—had it stuffed inside his shirt."

"Is that right, Vance?"

"Like I told her, I didn't mean no harm. I just wanted the picture, that's all. Your sister's a pretty woman."

Miranda's temper flared. "What are you, some kind of—"

"I'll take care of this, Miranda," Lucas said. "Go on back to the Rocking W. Your mom doesn't need any more excitement."

"No, she doesn't." She took a step toward Vance. "And if I find out you had anything to do with my sister's disappearance, you'll regret the day you were born."

"Well, there's nothing new in that!" he called after her.

With one final glare, Miranda got in her truck. She started to drive to the ranch, then abruptly changed her mind. Bypassing her normal route, she took the right fork in the road and gunned the engine. Vance

Porter might sell the best grass-alfalfa hay in the valley, but he was weird, not to mention a can or two short of a six-pack. And Miranda knew he had an eye for her mother. She'd seen the way he looked at Paige on the few occasions they'd run into him in town. Miranda trusted Vance about as far as she could throw him, especially after what she'd just witnessed. Why hadn't she thought to look at his place sooner?

He lived miles from town, at the end of a dirt road that wound up Cutback Mountain, in a cabin he'd built himself out of rough-hewn logs. Miranda hoped the guy planned to be in town for a while. With luck, Lucas would stall him, asking questions.

Two more Labradors rose from the porch to bark at her as she parked—a black one and a chocolate, its sun-faded coat cinnamon colored. "Hey, fellas," Miranda let the dogs sniff the back of her hand, then gave them a rub across their necks and behind their ears. They quickly decided she was a friend and followed her, tails wagging, as she climbed onto the porch. Miranda peered through the window beside the front door, but couldn't see much through the dusty glass and half-drawn curtains.

Making her way around the back of the cabin, she studied the pair of outbuildings in the cluttered yard. One looked like a toolshed, the other a makeshift garage. "Shannon!" she called, her voice bouncing off the hillside. If her sister was here, she would surely hear her. Miranda scanned the surrounding trees, and called again, with no answer except the whistle of a red-tailed hawk, gliding low in the sky.

Gripping the sheathed hunting knife she'd brought from the glove box, Miranda crept through knee-high grass and weeds toward the toolshed. She tried the door, but it was locked. One small window at the back let in a stingy amount of light, but again, the glass was so dusty and covered with cobwebs, she couldn't make out much. She had more luck with the garage.

The double door slid open easily on its track to reveal an oil-stained dirt floor. The place smelled musty, like damp wood and old car parts. A classic Ford pickup—Miranda would guess it to be a 1950-something model—sat on blocks, four tires that had seen better days propped around it. The truck was dark blue, lightly coated with dust, a few finger-prints on the fender, hood and door. A canvas tarp covered the bed, and Miranda's heart hammered, echoing inside her ears.

She moved in for a closer look. The tarp had been moved recently. Were the prints on the truck small enough to be Shannon's? Had Vance taken her away in this old pickup, then put it up on blocks to make it look as if the truck didn't run? Miranda reached for the ropes on the tarp, her fingers working to free the knot.

"What the hell do you think you're doing?"

Swallowing a yelp, she whirled around to face

Vance. The man looked angry, and taller than he had in town.

And in his broad hands he clutched the thick handle of a heavy-looking, sharp-bladed ax.

CHAPTER SIX

"I DIDN'T THINK YOU could sneak up on an Indian," Vance said. "Not unless you happen to be another Indian." He narrowed his eyes. "Lakota Sioux—on my daddy's side."

Miranda swallowed her fear, angry with herself for not hearing his truck pull into the yard. "Lay that ax down," she said, her gaze holding his. "Slowly." Damn! She'd been stupid to come up here like this. What had she been thinking?

That Shannon needed her.

It was all that had mattered.

To her annoyance, Vance chuckled. "What're you gonna do? Stick me with that buck knife you've got sheathed in your belt there afore I can chop up your gizzard with this?" He hefted the ax, and Miranda could see the silver glint of steel where the blade had been sharpened many times.

"I learned to throw a knife before I was old enough to recite the alphabet. I can pin a grasshopper to a dandelion stem faster than you can pop a top on a cold beer. So lay that ax down, and don't make me tell you again."

Vance shrugged. He couldn't quite erase his crooked smile as he leaned the ax against a toolbox. "You think I took your sister, don't you?"

"Maybe. Maybe not. You tell me."

He snorted. "And why would I be stupid enough to do that, if I had taken her?"

Miranda felt for the buck knife at her thigh for reassurance. "You wouldn't, which is why I came to have a look for myself. Why do you hide away in this cabin, anyway?"

He rested one booted foot on an open tackle box that held more fishhooks and lures than the local hardware store, and pulled a pouch of tobacco from his shirt pocket. "I don't like people," he said. "At least, not most of 'em." He smirked. "You, now…you I could learn to like. Spitfire that you are."

"You said you know my mom," Miranda said calmly, though her heart still raced. She still wasn't sure if Shannon was tucked away inside that dark cabin somewhere. "She's never acted like she knows you."

"She'd have no call to," Vance said, neatly tucking a pinch of tobacco inside his cheek, his brown fingers deftly rolling the foil pouch closed again. "I was a year behind her in school, plus I dropped out in the tenth grade. But I remember pretty Paige, with her black hair and those big ole brown eyes." He shook his head. "I hated that she hooked up with your daddy. He never was no account."

"I won't argue with you there," Miranda said. "What's under that tarp?"

Vance eyed the Ford as though he'd never seen it before. "Just a body or two," he muttered. "Well, the heads, anyway. Have a look for yourself, seeing as how that's what you'd aimed to do."

Miranda kept an eye on the man as she went to work at the knotted ropes once more.

"Here, let me help you."

She jumped when Vance stepped up beside the old truck, but if he noticed, he gave no indication. In tandem, they undid the ropes, and the burly man flipped the canvas back with one flick of his wrist. Miranda swallowed another scream at the sight of the glass eyes of two mounted deer heads among a scattering of items in the pickup bed. Most of it looked as though it had been there for quite a while.

"Told you," Vance said, laughing out loud.

Miranda almost smiled. "You going to show me around, then? I want to make sure my sister's not tied up somewhere in your cabin."

"Come on." Vance motioned for her to follow, and Miranda saw a jagged, white scar along the back of his hand. "I only tie my women up on Tuesdays, so you'll have to come back in a couple of days if that's what you're aiming to see."

"Not funny."

"Well, I haven't had much practice at tellin' jokes, seeing as how these dogs don't appreciate my sense of humor any more than you do." He opened the cabin door. "Go ahead and look. I'm going to put my supplies away." He tossed her a key. "Check the shed while you're at it. Maybe Ted Bundy's holed up in there or something."

"He's dead."

"Well, there you have it. More bodies for you to poke at. Maybe your sheriff friend can have a look-see while he's here." Vance jerked his chin in the direction of the dirt road just as Miranda heard the sound of tires on gravel.

She turned and saw Lucas in his Blazer, a scowl on his face she could spot even from this distance.

He parked behind her truck. "Now, how did I know you'd be here," he said, getting out. He stood with one big hand cocked against his hip, reminding her of an Old West cowboy about to draw his gun.

"Someone had to check. Heaven knows you couldn't have questioned Vance for more than a minute, as fast as he got back home."

"Don't tell me how to do my job."

"And don't tell me what to do." She tossed the shed key to him, and he caught it deftly. "Here. You want to be in charge, search the shed."

"Any evidence I found wouldn't stick without a search warrant."

"He gave me permission to look—you, too."

Lucas's scowl deepened. "Miranda, you know what I'm saying. You don't have any business being here." He lowered his voice a notch—barely. "Suppose Vance *was* dangerous...what then?"

"Then I guess you'd be investigating a stabbing about now. If he didn't ax me first."

Lucas stared at the knife hanging from her belt. "I'm not even going to tell you how much trouble you could get into for carrying that thing. I came up here to let you know we've got a lead, and this time I think it might be legitimate."

Miranda's breath stuck in her windpipe. "What? When?" she gasped.

"A woman called a few minutes ago, and she didn't sound like a crackpot. She supposedly saw Shannon with a guy on a motorcycle at the Gas-N-Go in Silver Creek last night. When the woman saw her picture in the news, she called in.

"She saw Shannon with a guy? Do you think this has something to do with Shannon's phone call the other night?"

"I was headed out that way when I realized you'd probably come up here."

"What are you waiting for? Let's go."

"There's no need for you to come. If the tip pans out, I'll call you."

Miranda let out a dry laugh. "I don't think so, cowboy. Shannon's not just my sister, she's my best friend. You can bet your sweet butt I'll be there anytime, anywhere there's even a hint of a lead."

"Let us do our job," Miranda. You could inadvertently destroy evidence, get in the way...bungle this case. Please." He turned and walked toward Vance's dilapidated toolshed.

"Lucas!" Miranda hurried to catch up, then gave his elbow a tug. At the feel of familiar, hard muscle, she pulled her hand away. "Go, then. I'll look in the shed."

"Miranda, go home. Paige shouldn't be alone. She looks like death warmed over."

She bristled at his condescending attitude. "Did you call her? She would really want to know about the tip."

"I'm not going to get her hopes up until I have something concrete to tell her. Now go on."

Ignoring him, Miranda set her jaw and continued walking. She heard him mumble something under his breath but chose to ignore it.

The shed turned out to be cluttered, but there was no evidence her sister had been there. Miranda stared at the shelves and boxes of junk.

"What about Vance's cabin? We should look before you go."

"Just chill, okay?"

She glared at him. *Hurry up, for pity's sake.*

After relocking the shed, Lucas headed for the modest log house, and knocked before entering. Miranda peered through the screen, having no real desire to go in unless she had good reason. Let Lucas look, since he'd gone all macho-professional on her. She heard him speak briefly with Vance, and minutes later, the two came back out on the porch.

"She's not here," Lucas said.

"Told you so." Vance smirked.

"I'll call you later," Lucas added.

Miranda started to argue, then shut her mouth and got in her truck. She refused to look at him as he backed out. Then she gave him thirty seconds before she followed him. She knew exactly where Silver Creek was, a town not much bigger than Sage Bend.

It might be Lucas's job to investigate, but she wasn't about to sit and wait. No way was she going to play damsel to this white knight.

LUCAS GLANCED IN HIS rearview mirror, already knowing what—or rather whom—he would see. *Damn, but Miranda was hardheaded.* He watched to see if she'd take the turnoff toward the Rocking W, but as he'd suspected, she followed him to the main highway.

Flipping on his lights, Lucas made a U-turn and headed back to the parking lot of the Truck Inn. Miranda drove up beside him and rolled down the passenger window of her Chevy. "What are you doing?"

"If you're going to follow me, you might as well park that thing and ride with me."

"I thought you'd never ask." She eased forward an inch, then braked. "This better not be a trick, Lucas, because if you drive off without me while I'm parking, I'll be back on your tail so fast you'll have to turn around and give me a ticket."

"No doubt."

She smiled smugly, found a spot for her pickup and was in the passenger seat of his Blazer before he could question his judgment.

Did he really have a choice?

"You ought to consider joining the force," he grumbled. "You're like a dog with a steak bone."

"You're just noticing that?" She buckled her seat belt. "Tell me more about this woman who called in. Did you get her name?"

"Anonymous caller—came from a phone booth in Silver Creek."

"What exactly did she say?"

"She supposedly saw Shannon with a guy on a motorcycle at the Gas-N-Go."

"With a guy? Do you think this has something to do with Shannon's phone call the other night?"

"I don't know. The woman gave a pretty fair description of Shannon. But of course, she might've seen her picture on the news and made the whole thing up. It happens, as you know."

He didn't want to give Miranda false hope. He probably shouldn't have even told her about the call in the first place, but he'd had to do something to make her leave Vance Porter's place.

"I can't stand watching the news anymore." She swatted at a buzzing fly. "Mom's obsessed with watching it, listening to it. She's got two TVs tuned to different stations, plus the radio's on in the kitchen. It's enough to give me a migraine."

Clearly, Miranda was hurting. He wanted to reach over and lay his hand on her arm. Give her some sort of comfort.

But he couldn't.

"I guess that's Paige's way of coping."

"I suppose. Me, I've got to do something more active. Sitting around waiting for the phone to ring is making me squirrelly."

"I never would've guessed."

Lucas stared at the road ahead. The thirty-five miles to Silver Creek was likely to feel like thirty-five hundred.

Leaving the siren off, he used his lights to speed their progress, praying the phone-in tip was legitimate.

"Since the caller was anonymous," Miranda said, "how will you know who to question?"

"Anyone and everyone around the Gas-N-Go."

Fifteen minutes later, he pulled into the parking lot. He'd been here before on more than one occasion, when he'd stopped to buy salmon eggs on his way to one of the best fishing holes he knew of, five miles north of Silver Creek.

A cowbell rang above the door when he and Miranda walked in.

"Hey, Sheriff." A burly man with thinning red hair and a neatly trimmed beard and mustache greeted him. "What brings you to our neck of the woods? You don't look dressed to fish."

"Nope. I'm hoping you can help me out, Scott."

"Sure, any way I can."

"We're looking for my sister," Miranda blurted. "She's been missing from our ranch in Sage Bend since Friday."

Lucas pursed his lips, trying to hold on to the last of his patience.

"I heard about that on the news," Scott said. "I'm awful sorry, ma'am."

Lucas pulled one of Miranda's flyers from his vest. "Somebody put a call in to my dispatcher from your pay phone—said they'd seen Shannon here yesterday evening. Do you know anything about that?"

Scott shook his head. "That's news to me. But I wasn't working yesterday. You might want to talk to my nephew Brad, and see if he noticed who all used the phone. Not that many folks do, most people having cell phones these days. Brad pulled a double shift, on account of my regular guy being sick."

"Where can I find him?"

Scott gave directions to Brad's house. "You can't miss it," he added. "It's painted a bright turquoise—only one in town that color." He chuckled. "Folks around here call it the Smurf house. Pisses my sister off something fierce, since she picked out the paint." He gave Miranda a sheepish smile. "Pardon my French, ma'am."

"Thanks, Scott." Lucas touched the brim of his hat. "I'll see you next time I'm down fishing."

"You do that. I sure hope you find your sister, ma'am."

"So do I. Is it all right if I put up a couple of flyers?"

"You bet."

Miranda taped one to the window and one to the ice machine. Outside, she wasted no time getting back into the Blazer. "Speaking of cell phones, have you found anything on Shannon's records, or Mom's phone?"

Lucas shook his head. "Nothing useful."

"What about the call Shannon got last Friday night?"

"It came from an unknown caller. Could be a blocked number or a disposable cell phone. Those can't be traced, but I am going to check with all the stores in this area that sell them. Matter of fact, I've got Garrett started on that today. I'll catch whichever ones he doesn't get to."

Miranda let out a palpable sigh. "Talk about looking for a needle in the old haystack."

"True enough." Lucas glanced at her. And wished he hadn't. In that moment, she looked young and vulnerable, reminding him of the twenty-year-old he'd left at the altar. A woman barely past being a girl.

He *hadn't* meant to hurt her.

But that girl was gone the instant Miranda caught his eye. The hard gaze of a woman used to toughing things out on her own stared back at him.

"I'm going to find her," she said. "No offense to your abilities as a sheriff."

"None taken." He wasn't offended, just concerned. He didn't want Miranda running foolish risks, getting herself into trouble too deep to get out of. "But you need to let me and my deputies handle this. You can help by sitting near the phone, in case Shannon calls. Your mom's at the ranch, but what about your place? Have you got anyone there, besides those cantankerous dogs of yours?"

"I hadn't given that much thought," Miranda said. She slammed her fist against the Blazer's door panel, startling him. "Damn it, I can't be three places at once. I want to be with Mom, I want to be out looking for Shannon..." She let the words trail away.

"What about your barrel racing students?" he asked. If he could get her to stay busy, she'd also stay out of his hair—and safe. He didn't dare tell her his suspicions about Lonnie Masterson. She'd probably end up at his jailhouse door, knowing Miranda. And Lucas already had his hands full with the DA where Masterson was concerned.

"They understand," Miranda said. "I've already phoned most of them, and I'll call the others later today. I'm sure they've heard all about what's happened by now."

"Don't you need the money your clinic brings in?"

Her face reddened. "What concern is that of yours?"

He couldn't win for losing. "None."

She was right. He had no claims on Miranda, no right to tell her what to do or to try to protect her.

After all, he'd been the one to hurt her most. And for that, he'd never forgive himself.

CHAPTER SEVEN

MIRANDA SWALLOWED HER disappointment as they
headed back to Sage Bend. Brad the nephew had
turned out to be a kid barely old enough to have a job,
with a typical teenage attention span. He'd noticed
nothing important or out of the ordinary yesterday
evening, but had agreed to let them know if he saw
or heard anything that might be useful. Lucas had
also knocked on a few doors throughout the neigh-
borhood near the Gas-N-Go, showing Shannon's picture around, asking people if they'd seen her.

Nothing.

"You're awful quiet," Lucas said.

"Yeah, well, I'm awful frustrated."

"I know. So am I… Miranda," he said, his voice
softening. "I really do wish you'd try to relax as
much as is humanly possible under the circumstances. You don't need to be running around
playing cop."

"I haven't meant to, but I—"

"Let me finish." He frowned. "You can keep searching on horseback and with Kyle, right? The volunteers

we have aren't giving up yet. I know some of the people around Sage Bend will ride until hell freezes over, if that's what it takes."

She knew he was right. And she knew she was probably being a pain in the ass. "Lucas, I'm not stupid enough to get in the way of you doing your job. But I have to be...involved...or I'll lose it."

"I understand." His tone was that of a teacher running out of patience. "But *you've* got to understand, too, Miranda. I can't worry about you getting hurt or interfering with police procedure, and at the same time focus on locating your sister. What if Vance had done something to you. He's never broken the law as far as I know, but there's something about him that I don't like. And don't tell me you had your knife, because it's a safe bet he could've disarmed you."

She pressed her lips into a thin line. "He'd have gone down trying. But," she added as Lucas opened his mouth, "I see your point. I'll try to show restraint in the future."

"Good." But he looked skeptical.

He dropped her off at the truck stop a short time later. "I'll come up and ride with you as soon as I can. I've got to check out some other things, like Shannon's computer...maybe go over her phone records again to be sure I didn't miss anything."

"Thanks, Lucas." Suddenly Miranda felt drained. "I do appreciate everything you and Garrett and your other deputies are doing."

"Just our job. Hey, are you hungry? We could grab some lunch, as long as we're here."

Miranda shrugged. "Not really. But I guess I need to eat. I'm kind of tired of the truck stop, though." *Not the food.* She was tired of all the people staring at her.

"So, we'll go to the Silver Spur. They make a mean steak sandwich."

"That actually sounds pretty good." Before she could question her sense of judgment, Miranda climbed back into the Blazer, and they took off.

The bar side of the Spur was closed on Sundays, the sliding partition that divided the restaurant from the honky-tonk in place. To Miranda's relief, the Spur wasn't as packed as the Truck Inn. Relishing the peace, she slid into a booth across from Lucas.

They ordered, and in no time she was biting into her sandwich with relish. She'd done nothing more than pick at food lately, and she truly was more hungry than she'd realized.

"Hey, there, Miranda. Lucas. How're y'all doin'?"

"Hi, Lily," Lucas responded. Lily Tate was in her seventies, but no one would ever guess. She was a regular at the Spur, especially on all-you-can-eat rib night.

"Any word on your sister?" Lily's brow furrowed in sympathy.

Miranda swallowed an inward groan along with her bite of sandwich. The meat and bread seemed to stick in her throat. "Not yet," she said. Lily meant well by asking.

"Well, at any rate, it's good to see the two of you back together again. They say God never closes a door without openin' a window." The older woman beamed at them like a proud grandparent, then gave Lucas's arm a pat. "If I was twenty years younger, I'd be after your fella here myself. You two take care, now."

Lily walked away, leaving behind an uncomfortable silence.

"Sorry about that," Lucas mumbled, suddenly deeply interested in dousing his French fries with more salt.

"You know," Miranda said, "I think I'd better get home and check on Mom."

"You've barely touched your sandwich."

"I'll take it with me."

"Well, I don't want to eat mine cold, or ruin it by heating it up in a microwave. I hate those things. They make everything taste like melted cardboard."

"So eat." She waved at a young woman who was one of her barrel racing students. "Sissy Spangler's headed for the cash register. I'll buy her meal and give her gas money to take me home."

Lucas sighed and pushed his plate away. "I'll take you."

"No. I don't want to ruin your lunch." Miranda gestured to their waitress, then asked for a take-out box.

"It's not a problem," Lucas said, pulling out his

wallet. Miranda beat him to it, throwing a twenty on the table.

But it was a problem, and she could tell he was more than a little annoyed as they left, which made her annoyed as well. What right did he have to act like they were indeed the couple Lily Tate assumed them to be, behaving as though they were out on a date or something, and that she'd just spoiled it?

"It was your idea to go to lunch."

"And you accepted." Lucas pulled out of the parking lot. "I can't help what Lily Tate thinks. What does it even matter?"

"Because Lily can spread gossip around Sage Bend faster than Fae and Mae. She'll have the whole town thinking I've fallen into bed with you." As soon as the words were out, Miranda wanted to take them back.

He looked at her, and for a heartbeat his anger was replaced by a hunger she hadn't seen in his eyes for years...a hunger that had nothing to do with steak sandwiches.

"Would that be so horrible?" he asked quietly.

Her jaw dropped. "You're kidding, right?"

Lucas merely lifted a shoulder, his attention on the road.

Laughing without humor, Miranda faced forward. "Unbelievable. Why do men seem to think sex can solve everything?"

"I didn't say that." He paused. "But it can't hurt."

"Are you propositioning me?"

"Not if you've still got that knife at your hip." He looked at her out of the corner of his eye and grinned. "Come on. Lighten up, Miranda. I was only teasing."

"That's not funny."

"I just wanted you to relax. Forget about everything for a while."

"You mean forget that my sister is missing, maybe even…" She couldn't bring herself to finish the sentence. It ticked her off that he would think she could so easily brush thoughts of Shannon aside for a romp in the sack with him.

It was only a steak sandwich.

"You know that's not what I meant," Lucas said. "Would it hurt you to relax for an hour? You're starting to look as haggard as your mother. Go home and take a nap."

"Gee, thanks." She wanted to throttle him.

"I give up." He shook his head.

Miranda remained silent for the rest of the drive.

For the second time, Lucas dropped her off at the Truck Inn. But before she could climb out of the Blazer, he caught hold of her hand and tucked a twenty dollar bill in it.

"I already—"

"I know you did, and I appreciate it. Just take it."

"Fine. See ya." Still seething, Miranda veered away from her truck to the diner's entrance for a cup of Mae's coffee. Tori put it in a to-go cup, and promised to be back at the ranch once her shift ended.

Her best friend gave Miranda the boost she needed, more so than the coffee. Paper cup in hand, she got in her truck and drove to the Rocking W.

When she walked in the door, the TVs and radio were on as usual. But Paige was nowhere to be seen.

"Mom?" Miranda called as she went down the hallway. She poked her head into Paige's bedroom. The bed wasn't made, and her mother's nightgown was draped over a rocking chair beneath the window.

Miranda found her in the barn, saddling Snap.

"Mom, what are you doing?"

Paige's normally dark skin looking waxy and pale, her eyes puffy and lackluster. "What's it look like, silly? I'm saddling my horse."

"I can see that. Where are you going?"

Paige dropped both arms to her sides, her body language that of a woman who'd reached the end of her rope. "I'm looking for your sister. Now quit trying to coddle me and go get your own horse, or saddle one of mine."

Her mother wasn't herself. She was hurting, and tired and scared beyond words. "You need to go to bed. How much sleep have you had in the past couple of days?" Miranda asked.

"Enough to function. And you're one to talk, anyway. If these damn fumbling Barney Fifes can't find Shannon, then by God I'll find her myself." Abruptly, Paige covered her face with both hands and started to sob.

Miranda's jaw nearly dropped. Her mother rarely cried, and never like this. She was one tough Cherokee woman.

Awkwardly, Miranda touched her mother's arm, then pulled her into a hug. Paige's shoulders heaved, and her sobs grew silent in their intensity. Her tears dampened Miranda's T-shirt, and she bit down hard on her lip as her own eyes welled. She couldn't cry, too. Her mom needed her.

"You can't help Shannon if you're dog-tired."

"I know," Paige said, sniffing. "I'm just mad. I'm so screaming mad! Who would want to hurt Shannon?" Her features crumbled. "This has to have something to do with that scum Lonnie Masterson. I just know it."

"If it does," Miranda said, "Lucas will figure it out. And in the meantime, we'll keep looking. But I do wish you'd lie down for a while. I'm thinking I might take a nap myself."

Paige's shoulders slumped in resignation. "I was going to cover the rimrock, up above the valley." She pointed to the west, and Miranda knew exactly where she meant. She, too, had thought of riding some of the tougher, steeper trails high above Cutback Mountain, even though they weren't easily accessible. She didn't want to leave any stones unturned.

"We'll do it later. Now go on inside. I'll put Snap in her stall."

"Okay." Reluctantly, Paige took a step away from her mare, then staggered as though dizzy.

Miranda caught her by the elbow. "Lean on me."

Paige waved her off. "Take care of my horse."

"Don't be so stubborn, Mom."

Paige harrumphed. "I'm not helpless. Now, would you please let me be."

"Okay." Miranda let go, lifting her hands in surrender. Still, she watched to make sure Paige got inside before she went back to take care of Snap.

With the mare comfortable in her stall, munching a flake of hay, Miranda left the barn. She heard a vehicle on the road and turned to wave—a small-town, friendly gesture—and saw Lucas's green Blazer, the horse trailer hooked to it.

Not now.

She leaned on his open window once he'd brought the rig to a stop. "Hi."

"You ready to ride?" he asked. "Garrett's already got quite a few of the volunteers riding out by the lake."

"Actually, I was about to follow your advice and take a nap while Chet and Sam are escorting a group of dudes. I guess business must go on," she said bitterly.

"Well, even dudes can act as a few extra pairs of eyes, right?"

"I suppose. Hey, I thought you were going to look at Shannon's computer?"

"I decided I could do that later, after it gets dark. Right now we need to take advantage of what's left of daylight hours if we're going to search."

He decided. It seemed to Miranda he decided everything, including calling off their wedding. She bit her tongue in an effort to hold it. "Don't you ever take a day off?"

"A lawman is never really off duty," he said, climbing from the Blazer. "And it wouldn't matter. I'd be here, anyway. So, do you want to search or would you rather take a breather?"

"No. I'll sleep later. Let's ride."

"How's your mom?"

"Resting."

He nodded. "Hopefully, we'll have some good news for her soon."

But the look on his face told Miranda otherwise. "You think Shannon's dead, don't you?" It was hard to even voice the words, especially because, in the back of her mind, she'd been thinking the same thing.

Lucas paused, hand on the horse trailer's latch. He reached out and gently touched her cheek, and what she saw in his eyes had her hurting all over again.

Regret?

Possibly.

She flinched and took a step back, and that quickly, the moment was gone. Lucas lowered his hand. "I don't know, Miranda. Of course, I hope she's not, but I don't know what to think."

"Well, thanks for your brutal honesty." But she wasn't really angry with him. She was angry with herself, she realized. Lucas wasn't telling her anything she didn't already know.

"You asked," he said, entering the slant-load trailer to walk Cimarron out.

"It's my fault, you know. That Shannon is missing."

He stopped dead in his tracks. "What do you mean by that?"

"I knew something was wrong. She hadn't been acting right for a while now. She was so upset and scared over testifying against Lonnie Masterson." Miranda shook her head, tears burning her eyes. "I never should've let her ride off alone. I should've gone after her right away, whether she wanted me to or not."

"Miranda." Lucas moved to touch her again, then dropped his hand to his side. "It's not your fault at all. How could you know something like this was going to happen?"

"I don't know." She wiped the corners of her eyes with her knuckles, willing the tears to stop. "I just wish I hadn't let her down."

"You didn't. Look at you, searching to the point of exhaustion. You know, I can just leave Cimarron here for the night if you'd rather. That way you can get some rest and we can start out fresh first thing in the morning."

Miranda let her breath out, the tired, drained feeling returning. "Maybe that would be better. I'm so worn-out, I don't think I'd be much good, anyway. I've barely slept the past few days."

"I imagine not." He walked Cimarron toward the

stables, and Miranda directed him to a stall near Snap's. She got the gelding some hay, then turned to bid Lucas goodbye. She was still smarting from his comments earlier at the Silver Spur.

For a moment she couldn't think of anything to say. Then her foggy brain registered that Lucas was still doing everything he could for her despite their personal differences.

"Lucas, thanks."

"For what?"

"Everything. You're putting a lot of time into looking for Shannon."

He shrugged. "I told you, I'm doing my job."

She knew it was so much more than that.

For a moment she imagined being back with him, sitting on the creek bank beneath the cottonwoods. She could still remember what his kisses tasted like. Warm, sweet...

And then her nonfunctioning, sleep-deprived brain was reliving the moment for real as Lucas tilted her face up to his and kissed her. It was a light, gentle kiss. Nothing sexy. Nothing out of line. And still it was one of the best kisses she'd ever had.

Miranda opened her eyes as he pulled away. Biting her bottom lip, she stared at him. "What was that?"

"A kiss. Don't tell me it's been so long, you've forgotten what they are."

"Ha-ha."

His lips curved, and her pulse jumped. He hadn't

smiled at her like that in ages. "Get some sleep," he said. "I'll see you in the morning."

She stayed in the barn until she heard him pull away, out onto the road.

Because she couldn't bear to let him see the flush she knew was on her face.

She was glad Tori was coming over later. She could use her friend's shoulder. Would Tori think she was crazy to be making plans—yet again—with Lucas? Would she understand Miranda's irrational feelings?

She'd thought she was over Lucas for good.

She'd thought wrong.

CHAPTER EIGHT

LUCAS MADE COFFEE the next morning, then filled a canteen with cold water and chipped ice. He was sure this would turn out to be another long, hot day. No rain had fallen in over a week, and while that was a blessing for tracking, it did make for an endurance test in the saddle.

Banjo, Lucas's big gray tomcat, rubbed against his legs, purring so loudly the sound seemed magnified. Lucas gave him and the other cats breakfast, then grabbed a doughnut and a glass of milk.

By seven o'clock he'd arrived at the Rocking W, where he found Miranda outside. She looked better than she had yesterday. Somewhat rested, anyway. Who was he kidding? She'd look good to him no matter what. That was a problem. He couldn't wait until they found Shannon, because not only did he want to bring her home safely to her family, he wasn't sure how much more he could stand, being this close to Miranda.

He could always scout on his own and leave her to search by herself.

Not an option. He didn't want anything to happen to Miranda, too.

"Morning." He slung the canteen over his shoulder as he walked her way. He'd left his tack here at the ranch along with his horse.

"Hey," Miranda greeted him. But she wouldn't meet his gaze. Should he apologize for the kiss he'd so impulsively planted on her yesterday? It hadn't really been much of a kiss, but...

Pretend it never happened. "How's your mom doing?"

"She's fine. She's not up to riding today, but she insisted on going to my place to take care of my animals. I ended up staying the night here with her."

"I'm sure she appreciated the company."

"Are you ready to go?"

"Yep." He held up the canteen. "I brought ice water."

She nodded, then went to get her horse from the barn. Lucas followed, and a short time later they were saddled up and riding toward the rimrock country on the other side of Cutback Mountain. It was a long, sweaty ride, and Lucas would safely bet the temperature was already nearing eighty by the time they reached the next area on Paige's search grid.

"Any special reason your mom wanted to look up here?"

"Not really. I think she's just wanting to cover every possibility." Miranda's mouth turned downward. "This is an impossible task, isn't it?"

"Hey, don't give up hope. I've seen searches go on for weeks until the missing person was found."

"Dead or alive?" She stared grimly at him.

"To be honest, both." He nudged Cimarron closer to Ranger. "Think positive. We *will* find her."

Miranda nodded.

They set out on the steep, winding trail up the bare mountainside, riding single file along the narrow track. It went on for what seemed like forever before topping out at a flat spot, surrounded by timber.

The trail continued through the trees—mostly pine and spruce—and Lucas breathed in the fresh air, glad he'd been born and raised in Big Sky Country. Even under the circumstances, he couldn't help but appreciate the rugged beauty. Lost in thought, he was taken by surprise when Miranda's horse bolted into Cimarron's hind end at the sound of a gunshot. The peaceful silence was shattered. Birds flew squawking from the trees, and as Lucas reined in his spooked horse, he saw Miranda tumble from the saddle, landing at the horses' feet.

"Whoa! Whoa…" he said to the geldings as he swung to the ground. Lucas snatched Ranger's reins before the black had a chance to bolt and possibly trample her.

"Miranda, are you all right?" But before she could answer, another shot cracked the air, hitting a nearby tree. "Shit! Stay down. Move…over there!"

He pointed, indicating a cavelike indentation in nearby rock.

Without a word, Miranda did as he said, which meant she had to be as shook up as he was.

Lucas analyzed the hillside opposite them, in the direction the shots had come from. "Hey!" He shouted toward the trees. "There are riders down here! Can you hear me?" He paused. "This is Sheriff Lucas Blaylock. Do you *hear* me?"

The answer was a third shot.

"Damn it." Lucas scuttled as fast as he could toward Miranda's rocky shelter, tugging the horses along behind him. He coaxed the geldings into an area where the outer rocks safely blocked them from danger...he hoped.

"Who the hell is shooting at us?" Miranda snapped.

"How should I know?" He thrust the horses' reins at her. "Hold them." Drawing his 9 mm, he eased toward the opening in the rock face.

"Where are you going?" She laid a hand on his arm, but he shrugged it off.

"To see if I can arrest someone."

"Are you nuts? You don't know how many of them there are. Obviously, they're shooting at us on purpose."

"And obviously, it's my job to stop them." Ignoring her protests, Lucas eased back outside. Pausing, he listened. He didn't hear anything except a few outraged birds.

"You!" he called. "Show yourself. Now."

Of course, no one did. He hadn't really expected them to, unless the shooting had been an accident—misplaced target practice or something. But he knew better.

Lucas ducked back into the rock shelter. "You okay?"

"Nothing hurt but my pride. I was so busy looking around, I wasn't paying attention to my horse." She shook her head. "Ranger normally doesn't spook like that."

"Yeah, well, any horse can spook under the right circumstances."

"Now what do we do?" Miranda's eyes were wide, not so much with fright as with acute awareness.

"Wait it out. Keep alert." She was shaking. Lucas squeezed her shoulder. "You sure you're all right?"

"I'm not afraid of a lot of things, but that scared the hell out of me." She pressed a hand to her chest. "I thought for sure we were going to be shot."

"That makes two of us."

Forty-five minutes passed without incident, but Lucas kept his handgun at the ready. When another fifteen went by, he was confident it was safe to head on up the trail.

"My muscles are really starting to cramp," Miranda said, as though reading his mind.

Working out a charley horse, Lucas stood. "I hear you. Come on, let's ride. Just be alert." He holstered the 9 mm and took the lead. He'd gotten a bead on approximately where the shooter had been.

"Do you think whoever it was was trying to hit me or you?"

Lucas shrugged. "Who knows. Both of us, possibly…probably."

"Wonderful." He could hear the catch in her voice. "First they take my sister, now they're trying to kill us, too."

Lucas pulled up on his reins and turned in the saddle. "Hey. What did I tell you about thinking negatively? Whoever that was, they could've and probably would've killed us if that's what they intended to do. I think those shots were meant as a warning."

"I suppose. Unless whoever it was is just a lousy shot."

"I doubt it."

"So, the shooter was trying to scare us?"

"Most likely." Lucas faced forward. "Maybe we're getting close to Shannon."

MIRANDA'S HEART THUNDERED AT the possibility that Shannon could be somewhere nearby. Of course! Why else would someone be at this very spot, at this very moment, shooting at her and Lucas?

"There are several abandoned mines in this area, and a couple of line shacks," she told him. "Oh, man, why didn't I think of that before? Do you think Shannon could be hidden in one?"

"If so, we'll find out," he said over his shoulder. "I've already had my deputies search most of them."

Miranda stared at the back of his cowboy hat. Silver hat, close enough to white. Good guy.

Ha. She'd better stay focused on Lucas the lawman. Not Lucas the man. He wasn't so good as far as she was concerned.

A search of Lucas's target on the hillside opposite turned up little. Miranda spotted a disturbance of the grass and of some evergreen needles covering the ground, but no clear footprints. No brass shell casings, either, which meant the shooter had either picked them up or had fired a gun that didn't kick the brass out. But it had sounded like a .22 rifle.

By the time she and Lucas returned to the ranch, Miranda would safely bet they'd covered close to ten miles, including the rimrock and a good deal of the forested BLM land around it. The only thing they'd stirred up were a few deer and a small bachelor band of mustangs. Miranda had paused to watch the beautiful sight as the young horses sniffed the air, nostrils flaring when they scented Ranger and Cimarron and what must be to them the strange smell of humans. Then the half-dozen young stallions had turned and run, until the trees swallowed them up.

At the barn, Paige joined Lucas and Miranda as they unsaddled their horses.

"Any luck?"

Miranda gave Lucas a look. "Nothing yet, Mom."

She didn't want Paige to know about the gunshots. It would only worry her more.

"Keep your chin up," Lucas said. "We've got a lot of ground to cover yet."

Just then, his cell phone rang, and Miranda nearly jumped out of her skin. She hadn't realized just how much the shots fired at them had scared her. From now on, she'd be sure to pack the .44 when she went out searching, or her .357 magnum.

Engrossed in grooming Ranger, Miranda almost missed the look on Lucas's face. But when her mother's own face went pale, Miranda stared at him. Something was definitely wrong. He walked a few feet away, speaking quietly into the phone. They heard him say, "I'll take care of it."

He snapped the cell phone closed.

She knew. But she asked, anyway.

"What?"

"That was Garrett." Lucas paused, and his eyes said it all. "A woman's body was found about a half hour ago in Cameron County. She fits Shannon's description."

Miranda felt herself crumble, even as her mind registered her mother's wail. Dizzily, she staggered a half step, her vision beginning to blur.

This was not happening.

Lucas took hold of Miranda's elbow, then wrapped his arm around her waist. "Hold on," he said. "We don't know anything for sure yet."

Paige grabbed her hand and squeezed so hard, Miranda thought her bones would break. "What do you mean, 'We don't know anything yet,'" Paige raved. "She's dead! Oh, God. My baby girl is dead."

"Mom." Miranda slipped from Lucas's grasp and pulled her sobbing mother into her own shaking arms. "Shh. Lucas is right. We can't be sure it's Shannon."

"It is. I feel it." Paige let out another animal-like wail that curdled Miranda's blood.

"Mom, stop it!" She gave her a shake. "Stop it. You've got to get ahold of yourself."

"I'm sorry," Paige whispered, glancing at Lucas. "I'm really sorry. Look at me, falling all to pieces when I always taught you girls to be strong, no matter what."

"No need to apologize," Lucas said softly. "Try to keep your chin up until we know something for sure. Okay?" This last he said to Miranda as he squeezed her shoulder.

Out of reflex, she reached up and covered his hand with hers. "Wh-where is she?"

"The coroner's office. Garrett's headed that way."

"Not without me." Miranda lowered her hand.

"It's not necessary."

"The hell it's not." She turned to her mother. "Mom, I want you to go in the house and call Tori... Fae...someone. Have them come stay with you while I go with Lucas."

"I want to go, too," Paige said firmly. "Shannon is my daughter."

"And she's my sister and you're my mother, and I'm not about to let you identify... Just stay here, Mom. Please?"

At that moment, the past few days seemed to catch up with Paige. Her face turned a shade of gray that scared Miranda spitless. All she needed on top of everything else was for her mom to have a heart attack.

"Come on." Miranda took her mother into the house and steered her to a recliner, dissuading further argument. She spread a lightweight throw over Paige's lap.

Paige whipped the throw off. "Criminy, Miranda, it's eighty-some degrees outside! Are you trying to kill me?"

Taking a deep breath, Miranda leaned over and gave her mother a hug, and a kiss on the cheek. "Sit tight, Mom. I'll call you the minute... I'll call you when we get there."

"Fine." Paige sulked like a child. Miranda wondered when her mom had last slept.

Probably about the same time she had.

Receiver tucked between her chin and shoulder, Miranda phoned Tori, who'd already heard the news via the police scanner Fae and Mae had recently installed in the back room of the Truck Inn.

"My God, Miranda. I was just headed out the door to your place. Don't move an inch, I'm on my way."

"Tori—" But she'd already hung up. "Dang it all." Miranda couldn't wait for her. She had to leave now.

She pushed her way through the screen door, and stopped in her tracks on the porch. "Damn you, Lucas Morgan!"

His Blazer was no longer in the driveway.

No matter.

Miranda fired up her truck and sped after him. With Lucas and Garrett on their way to the coroner's office, leaving only Mac and Frank to take care of other duties, she had a fifty percent less chance of getting a speeding ticket.

Pressing her foot down on the accelerator, Miranda watched the speedometer climb, and tried not to picture her sister lying on a cold, steel table.

CHAPTER NINE

LUCAS WALKED THROUGH the halls of the Cameron County coroner's office looking for the right set of doors. He'd been here only once before, but he hated the place. The walls were painted a color that reminded him of pea soup someone had seen twice. Moving at a brisk pace—he knew Miranda would be close behind him—he found what he was looking for.

Pushing through the double doors into another smaller hallway, Lucas found Hal Sutherland's office door open. The guy couldn't be more than thirty years old, and Lucas wondered what would make a man his own age want to take a job like this.

"Sheriff Blaylock." Hal stood and held out a big-boned hand. "It's good to see you again, though I wish the circumstances weren't what they are."

"I hear you." Lucas shifted his weight, hating this part of his job, which, thank God, didn't come up often. The worst case had been a few years ago, when he'd had to witness an elderly woman identify her daughter and two grandchildren, who'd been killed by a bear.

"Might as well get it over with," Hal said, as though reading his thoughts.

Lucas went with him to the room at the end of the short hallway. Inside, two stainless steel tables and various saws and autopsy tools gave Lucas the heebie-jeebies. He wished Cameron County could afford video cameras for on-screen identification.

Hal paused in front of the row of steel drawers, and suddenly Lucas was filled with an intense sadness. If the woman inside this awful place was Shannon, Miranda was going to lose her mind. And if she wasn't, then some other poor family would have to face their loss.

"Ready?" Hal asked, hand on the drawer.

He nodded. "Go ahead."

Hal flipped the latch, then slid the steel table out and expertly folded the white sheet away from the woman's face. Lucas let out a breath he hadn't been aware of holding.

It wasn't Shannon.

Thank God.

Hearing voices in the hallway, he turned in time to see Miranda burst in—just ahead of Garrett—an older woman with a pinched face hot on their heels. "Miss, I told you, no one is allowed—"

"It's all right," Lucas said. "She's with me." He lowered his voice as he took hold of Miranda's shoulders in an attempt to block her view of the body.

She craned her neck, trying to see around him.

"It's not Shannon," he said. Still, he had to keep a firm grip on Miranda's shoulders before it finally registered and she stopped squirming.

"It's not? Are you sure?"

"Positive. I'd say that gal is about twenty years old, shorter than Shannon by a couple of inches." He didn't want to tell her that death often made faces unrecognizable, especially after a few days. Still, he'd seen enough to be sure.

"Thank God." Miranda covered her eyes, fighting back tears. "Who is she, I wonder?"

"I have no idea. Hopefully, Sheriff Runyon and the state police will figure it out. Excuse me a minute." Lucas stepped aside to speak to Garrett and two patrolmen who had just arrived—officers he'd worked with in the past. Carter and Hernandez.

"We're going to follow up on this," Hernandez said. "With Lonnie Masterson in jail, I don't really see a connection, but with the similarities, well, there's always a chance. Or it could be a copycat."

Lucas nodded. "I guess it's possible." This might give credence to Miranda's original suspicion that Shannon could be a victim of a copycat killer, especially since they hadn't found a connection to implicate Lonnie. Hal closed the drawer again.

"Sorry I couldn't be of any help," the coroner said. "But I'm glad our Jane Doe isn't your missing girl."

"Appreciate it." Lucas nodded. "If there's anything I can do, call me," he said to Hernadez and

Carter. "Tell Runyon I'm at his disposal, and that I'll call him later."

"Will do." Carter tugged at the brim of his hat. He and Hernandez and Garrett left the room.

Hal held the door open for them, and Lucas steered Miranda through, never so glad to leave a place in his life.

Outside, he marched her to her truck. The heated engine was still ticking from having been pushed to highway speed—and then some, if he knew Miranda. He turned her to face him, rubbing his thumbs against her arms. "What am I going to do with you?"

"I had to know."

"What, you don't think I would've told you?"

"I had to see for myself." She glared at him. "Why did you take off without me?"

"To spare you from what you just saw."

Her features softened, but only for a brief moment. "I don't want to be spared. Lucas."

The look on Miranda's face. The fire in her. That was what had attracted him to her in the first place. He gave her arms one last rub, then reluctantly lowered his hands.

"My shadow may end up cooling her heels in a jail cell overnight if she's not careful," he said. "How fast did you drive, coming here?"

"Obviously not quite as fast as you did."

"I'm a cop, remember?"

She merely narrowed her eyes, then climbed behind the wheel of the Chevy. "Goodbye, Lucas. Keep in touch."

"You know I will." He leaned on her open door, preventing her from closing it right away. "Drive safely."

"Will do." She gave him an innocent smile, and he couldn't help but chuckle as he watched her pull away.

MIRANDA DROVE AS FAST AS she dared back to her mom's place. Paige had fallen into an exhausted sleep in the recliner and didn't move when she came through the door. Miranda took a moment to study her face. She had dark circles beneath her puffy eyes, and her mouth was pinched and drawn, her muscles tense even as she slept. Miranda hated to wake her.

"Mom," she whispered. Paige shot up out of the recliner as if she'd been goosed.

"Shannon?" She looked around. "Miranda. Oh… I—I must've been dreaming." She blinked, obviously trying to clear her thoughts.

"It wasn't her, Mom." Miranda managed a smile. "The woman over in Cameron County isn't Shannon."

"Oh, dear Lord. Thank you." Paige pulled her into a hug. For the first time in days, Miranda felt her mom's strength as she gripped her.

"Are you positive? Did you…see her?"

Miranda nodded. She'd caught only a glimpse of the woman in the morgue, and it had been a sad, sad sight. One she'd never forget. How much worse if Jane Doe had been her sister.

"It's not her," she repeated.

Paige sat down again. "Then they don't know who the woman is?"

"Not yet. But the sheriff over there is on it." As sorry as she felt for that woman's family, Miranda's thoughts were on Shannon.

Where *was* her sister?

Square one didn't feel so good, after all. But at least Shannon might still be alive.

Clinging to that hope, Miranda fixed Paige something to eat. Her own stomach was still too unsettled for her to want anything.

"Where's Tori?" she asked.

"I guess she left when I fell asleep," Paige said. "She was kind of ticked you hadn't waited for her."

Miranda cringed. She'd have to call her friend and apologize. "Well, I couldn't wait."

"I know. She'll get over it. But you're not going to believe who called while she was here."

"Who?"

"Clint Blaylock. Said he wants to help with the search, and to call him the next time the group rides out."

"You're kidding me."

Paige shook her head.

"Well, that's something. I guess another pair of eyes can't hurt." Providing Clint could manage to stay sober. She wondered how Lucas would feel about him getting involved.

After making sure her mom didn't need anything else, Miranda drove home. Tuck and Smudge greeted her with their usual enthusiasm.

Miranda grabbed a Coke from the fridge, then dialed Tori's cell phone.

"You're in trouble," her friend said without preamble.

"Tori, I'm sorry. But I couldn't wait one more second to see if it was Shannon."

"Okay. You're forgiven, especially since I already heard through the grapevine that it wasn't."

Miranda rolled her eyes. "I can't believe how fast gossip travels around here."

"Well, you know how it is. Telephone, text message or tell Fae and Mae."

Miranda chuckled. "I thought that went 'Telephone, telegraph…'"

"Tele-what?" Tori said. She was three months younger than Miranda, and milked that for all it was worth. "Seriously, I'm so glad it wasn't Shannon."

"No kidding." Miranda sipped her Coke, sitting back on the couch with the dogs at her feet. "I'm going to go nuts if we don't find her soon."

"I'm sorry," Tori said. "I wish there was something more I could do to help."

"I appreciate that."

"Hey, did your mom tell you that Clint called and offered to help?"

"Yeah. Maybe Lucas got through a little."

"Maybe, but I wouldn't hold my breath. It's more likely he's trying to get on Dena's good side again. He ought to loan her his horse and let her come out and ride. Give her a break from the kids for a while. I don't think the poor thing gets to go much of anywhere."

"Not that I've seen." Miranda sighed. "I wonder if Lucas found anything on Shannon's computer yet. He hadn't the last time I asked."

"Well, keep me posted," Tori said. "I'm always here if you need me."

"Thanks, babe."

Miranda hung up and made her way to the kitchen. She supposed it was relief that had brought back her appetite, despite her earlier queasiness at the coroner's office. With Smudge and Tuck eyeing her hopefully, Miranda slapped together a ham sandwich and chips. She munched automatically, tossing the dogs scraps of food as she sat at the table, lost in thought.

If Lucas couldn't find Shannon, and Miranda couldn't find her, what in world were they going to do? She picked up the phone again, this time to call Sissy Spangler. The daughter of one of Fae's closest friends, Sissy was a slip of a girl who always seemed swallowed up by her saddle as she rounded the barrels on her big quarter-Thoroughbred cross.

Sissy lived a couple of miles away, and usually rode her gelding over to practice barrels, sometimes daily. She would be a senior when school started back up again in August, and Miranda had the feeling

Sissy was going places. She was smart, and one hell of a horsewoman.

"Sissy, hi. It's Miranda."

"Miranda." Loud and vivacious, Sissy's voice and mannerisms didn't fit her tiny frame one bit. "Omigod, are you doing okay? Any news on Shannon?"

"Not yet."

"I heard the sheriff thought they might've found her de…found her over in Cameron County."

"It wasn't her."

"I heard. I'm so relieved."

"Anyway, Sissy, I was wondering if you'd like to come over and run some barrels. I need to get my mind off…things."

"Sure." Sissy perked right up. She lived to ride, reminded Miranda of herself ten years ago.

Something in her had changed after Lucas left. She'd turned to rodeo and riding as a means of escape, rather than a source of pleasure. "All right then. See you in a little while."

Miranda hung up, then went outside to saddle the roan she'd been training for Shannon. If her sister came back and found her horse out of shape, she wouldn't be very happy. Miranda saddled the red roan—Sangria—and warmed her up in the arena.

Miranda was running the barrel pattern at a lope when Sissy trotted up the driveway on Scoot. She wore faded jeans tucked into her gray cowboy boots, a barrel racing bat poking up from the right one. Her teal-colored T-shirt brought out the turquoise in her eyes, and her shoulder-length, pale-blond hair was plaited into a single braid beneath a ball cap that read Barrel Racer, Cowboy Chaser.

"Hey, Miranda." Sissy pulled Scoot to a halt outside the arena fence. "Sangria's looking good."

"Thanks." She swung down from the saddle and led the mare over to the fence. "I thought I'd keep her tuned for Shannon."

"I'm sure she'll appreciate it." Sissy met her gaze head-on. "I've been riding with the search groups, you know, every chance I get. In addition to the formal search the county had mounted, many neighbors were riding out catch as catch can around their nine-to-five work schedules. We're going to find her."

"I know." Miranda managed a smile. "Now let's get started on that big brute of yours."

Sissy laughed. "You're not a brute, are you, baby?" She stroked the neck of the sixteen-hand-plus chestnut, then rode into the arena.

When the training session was over, Miranda felt relaxed for the first time in days. She was ready for a hot shower. Afterward, she called to check on her mom, who assured her she was hanging in there. Paige turned down her offer to come sleep at the Rocking W.

"Stay home, honey. I think we both need some time alone with our thoughts. Plus Chet and Sam are out in the bunkhouse if I need them."

"Okay. If you're sure."

Miranda slipped into an oversize T-shirt, put a movie in her DVD player and settled on the couch with a cold beer and popcorn, which she shared with Tuck and Smudge. But the movie could've been about anything as far as she was aware of it. The beer made her sleepy, and within minutes she dozed off on the couch. She slept fitfully, too tired to go to bed, yet unable to sleep well.

It was the dogs who woke her. Smudge ran to the door, and Tuck put his paws up on the living room windowsill. Ears perked, he searched the yard, then suddenly threw his head back and let out an ear-splitting bark.

Instantly, Miranda was alert. She flew to the kitchen in her bare feet and reached into a utility drawer for the loaded gun she kept there. One in the kitchen, one in her bedroom. A woman living alone in the boonies couldn't be too careful. With the .357 Smith and Wesson in hand, she crept to the living room, sidling up against the wall. Smudge had joined Tuck at the window and the two continued to bark like mad.

Cautiously, Miranda parted the back side of the curtain then cursed. Lucas stood on her lawn, in plain view beneath her yard light. She lowered the revolver.

Jerking the door open, Miranda commanded Smudge and Tuck to stay, then stomped outside. "What are you doing lurking out here in the dark? Lucas, you scared the hell out of me."

"I wasn't lurking, and I was standing under the light."

"Did you ever hear of knocking?"

"I wanted to make sure those two hellhounds of yours weren't out here waiting to waylay me. Then I saw one at the window, and I thought it might be wise to make sure he didn't come through the glass."

"Why are you here?" Her gut churned. "Oh—is something wrong? Did you hear something about Shannon?"

"No," he said hastily. "I just came by to check on you. You've had a hell of a day."

"Same one you had."

He grunted, then his gaze fell to the pistol she still held, half tucked in the folds of the oversize T-shirt. At the same time, Miranda realized what she was wearing, and tugged at the hem with her free hand, hoping her practical cotton underwear wasn't showing.

"What's that?" Lucas pointed, and Miranda purposely chose to misunderstand.

"An extra-large T-shirt. I sleep in them."

"The pistol!" he said impatiently. "What in thunder are you doing with what I'll assume is a loaded gun?"

Miranda looked down at the revolver as though it were an afterthought, just a part of her hand.

"Well, now, it wouldn't do me much good if it weren't loaded, would it?"

CHAPTER TEN

LUCAS DID HIS BEST to hold on to what was left of his patience. As if he didn't have enough to worry about, he now had to contend with an armed, jumpy woman.

"It's not going to do you any good when you end up shooting off your own foot with that gun."

Miranda glared at him, her face dark red. "I've been target shooting since I was in elementary school."

"Do you have any idea how many home owners are shot—often killed—with their own guns?"

"You know what you can do with your statistics," she snapped.

"Miranda…"

"Do you want to come in or would you rather stand out here skulking in the moonlight?"

"I wasn't skulking, either."

"Whatever."

Suddenly, she burst into tears. Lucas couldn't have been more surprised if she'd spontaneously combusted. Like her mom, Miranda was tough, and he'd rarely seen her cry.

He wondered if she'd cried the day he'd stood her up.

"Miranda." He stepped forward and put his arm around her shoulder, and she let out a sob that had him gathering her against his chest. "Shh," he soothed. "It's going to be all right." He pried the gun from her hand and laid it on the hood of her truck.

"I can't take any more," she said. "I just can't."

"Yes, you can." He tilted her chin up, forcing her to look into his eyes. "You're going to get through this no matter what."

More tears squeezed out and slid down her cheeks. "No matter if my sister ends up like that poor woman in Cameron County? I don't think so."

"That's not what I meant." But really, he had. He wanted to believe they'd find Shannon alive and well, but the more time that passed, the more he had his doubts. The lawman in him would not let go of statistics. "We're going to find Shannon, and she's going to be fine. She's tough, too."

"I feel helpless and useless and furious...and it makes me so damn frustrated!" Miranda struck her fist against his shoulder—not hard, but hard enough.

"Hey, take it easy."

Her blue eyes, now red with tears tore his heart out. Lucas kissed her without a second thought. At first he brushed his lips lightly over hers, and she stiffened slightly. But when she kissed him back, it was all over for him. He took her mouth, kissing her deeper and deeper, lacing his tongue around hers. She tasted so sweet, like rainwater after a dry spell. Like a cold beer after a hot ride.

Lucas grew hard. He wanted Miranda now, beneath him on the grass. Pushing her shirt up, he kneaded her breasts, moaning when he confirmed she wore no bra.

"Lucas," she whispered. "We shouldn't be doing this."

"Shush." He smothered her protest with his mouth. She kissed him back, rubbing his shoulders, running her hands up and down his back until he thought he'd lose his mind. He had the wild urge to move her hands much lower. Instead, he scooped her up into his arms and carried her inside to the bedroom, kicking the door shut in the startled faces of her dogs.

Her gaze met his and he could see a challenging sparkle in her eyes. There was nothing tender in the look she gave him, and there was nothing tender about the way she tore off his clothes when he laid her on her bed in the darkened room.

Her aggression both surprised and pleased him. This wasn't the young woman he remembered. Miranda was grown, mature, and she obviously knew what she wanted as she threw her own clothes off, then pushed him back onto the bed and straddled him.

"I'm going to make you want me like you've never wanted anyone, anything, in your life."

"Mission accomplished." He chuckled.

But his laughter quickly faded when he saw how serious she was. She leaned over him. "Shut up and kiss me." She locked her mouth over his, their tongues tangling.

He wasn't about to argue.

FIRE COURSED THROUGH HER veins as Miranda kissed Lucas. He felt good beneath her, his muscles solid and as hard as the rimrock they'd explored earlier. She wanted to dominate him...wanted to make him hurt the way he'd hurt her.

Sitting back, she rubbed against his groin, teasing him, refusing to let him enter her. "Not yet," she growled. She was going to give him something he'd never forget. Make him want what he couldn't have.

With her hands against his chest, she wriggled and shimmied, sending him a saucy look. Leaning down, she kissed him, over and over. She let her tongue tease his, let her lips devour him. Then she worked her way down his body, kissing, nibbling, tickling him with the tip of her tongue, until she reached his erection. He was so hard, she wondered if he would last. Tracing the base with her tongue, she took pleasure in the deep moan she elicited.

Stroking him, she worked her way upward, then took him into her mouth. As she slid her tongue around the tip of his erection, he moaned and thrust his hips against her. Then he tugged her into his arms and rolled her over on the bed.

"I wasn't finished with you," she protested.

"Maybe not, but you were about to finish me off." His lips curved, and he pinned her beneath him. "My turn."

Bending, he kissed her neck, licking a path to her ear. Now she moaned as he traced her ear, then took her mouth in a frenzied kiss. She tried to remind herself she'd wanted to make him crazy, not the other way around. But everything he did to her felt so good, it no longer mattered. With a growl, she wrapped her legs around him and allowed him to slide inside of her.

And nearly cried out with the pleasure of it.

Lucas felt so good, so wonderfully familiar. And yet different. Her young lover, just a few years past boyhood, had matured into a man who knew exactly what he wanted. And for the moment, that was her.

They made love twice, then lay in each other's arms. Miranda draped one hand across Lucas's chest, leaning her head against his shoulder.

"That was phenomenal."

He chuckled. "I've never been called phenomenal before, but I think I'll second that."

She smacked him. "I didn't mean *you* were phenomenal, I meant *we* were." As soon as the words left her mouth, she regretted them.

Lucas stroked her hair. "Yeah," he said, his voice husky, serious. "We are."

Abruptly, the room filled with tension. As gently as possible, Miranda extracted herself from his grasp. "I really ought to be getting to sleep," she said. "Tomorrow's another long day."

He took the hint. "That's for sure." Rising, he gathered his clothes.

Miranda admired his backside as he stepped into a pair of charcoal-colored boxer briefs, then his blue jeans and chambray shirt. He turned to face her, and she averted her gaze. She'd already slipped back into her T-shirt and panties.

Miranda could not bring herself to look up. "I guess we had some pretty hot sex, but that doesn't mean…"

"I never assumed it did," Lucas said. "Good night, Miranda. Don't forget your gun." He put on his cowboy hat and stepped out into the hall.

Immediately, Smudge and Tuck heeled him. Miranda heard him curse, and the sound of boot heels clacked against her hardwood floor in hurried steps. Miranda couldn't help it. She let out a chuckle, then called off the dogs. Padding barefooted down the hallway, she paused and leaned in the living room doorway.

But Lucas didn't look back as he left.

FOR THE NEXT THREE DAYS, Miranda made herself scarce. Making love with her might have been a mistake, yet somehow it had felt right. Lucas wasn't sorry about it, so long as he hadn't hurt her again.

Though they'd both gone out with a search party the day before, Miranda had ridden out earlier, taking a different region.

To Lucas's surprise, Clint had insisted on coming along. His brother had sworn he was off the booze as of two days ago, and that he was turning over a new leaf. Sadly, it was the umpteenth time Lucas had heard that same story. He'd spent part of the ride trying to talk Clint into counseling, to no avail.

"I can stand on my own two feet," he insisted. "I may be a drunken jackass sometimes, but I love Dena and my boys. I'm going to do right by them. You'll see."

Lucas wished he could believe him.

Now as he answered a call dispatch put through to his desk, he did his best to clear his mind. "Blaylock," he said.

"Lucas, this is Carrie Hopkins. How're things going on your end?"

Carrie worked for the DA's office in Sage County and was a whiz with computers. When Lucas hadn't been able to find anything on Shannon's computer, he'd turned it over to her.

"About the same. Did you find anything?"

"Not much, but there is a deleted e-mail I think you'd be interested in. I've already forwarded it to you."

"What's it say?"

"Read it. Call me back if you have any questions, but I doubt I'll be much more help to you."

"Okay. Thanks, Carrie." Curious, he hung up and rolled his desk chair to the computer. After logging on, he searched his in-box. There.

Lucas clicked on the e-mail, read it and felt his stomach turn over.

Tori, thanks for helping me. You can't know how much I appreciate it. You're a good friend. TTYL—Shannon.

The e-mail was dated the twenty-first of June, just a couple of days before Shannon had disappeared.

Picking up the phone, Lucas dialed the diner.

"Truck Inn, Mae speaking."

"Mae, it's Lucas. Is Tori there?"

"Nope. She's off today. Would you like her cell number?"

"Please." He scrawled it on his desk blotter, thanked Mae, then hung up before she could start asking questions.

Tori sounded half-asleep when she answered the phone, even though it was nearly noon. He supposed she worked odd hours, dividing her time between the diner and the Spur. "Tori, it's Lucas. Can you come down to my office?"

"Now?" she mumbled.

"If you don't mind."

He heard her yawn heartily. "Sorry. Sure, Lucas.

Is it Shannon? Did you find something?" Now she sounded worried.

"I'd rather wait and talk about this when you get here."

"Okay. I'll be right there."

Lucas hung up and poured himself a cup of coffee. His umpteenth since he'd woken up that morning. And for the umpteenth time, his thoughts turned to making love with Miranda. She'd felt so soft and warm beneath him. And she'd been such a hellion... Just thinking about it turned him on. Yet she hadn't called him, hadn't come by. Instead, she checked in for news with Garrett every day.

And when most of the rescue workers had pretty much given up, she'd continued the search...with Kyle Miller. It was none of Lucas's business. He and Miranda had made love, but that didn't mean they were back together. On the contrary, when Miranda had dismissed him that night, it had felt more like "Goodbye, Johnny" than a new step in their relationship.

Who was he kidding? There was no relationship. Not anymore.

While he waited for Tori, he busied himself with looking over a topographical map of the area where Shannon had disappeared. Where could she be? So many hills and valleys...

Minutes later, Tori knocked on the open door of his office. She was dressed in jeans and a bright yellow shirt, her hair sprayed big as usual.

"Come on in." He gestured. "You want some coffee?"

"Are you kidding? I get so much of that stuff at the diner, I'm pretty sure I'm blood related to Juan Valdez." She took a seat. "So, what's up?"

He slid the printout of the e-mail in front of her and watched her face go white, then red. She looked up, meeting his gaze. "I can explain."

"Go ahead."

"Well, um, Shannon met a guy online a few months ago. She tried to break it off with him, but… I had to go online and help her out. Tell him to let it go."

Lucas felt his temper go from zero to fifty in the span of seconds. "You— Tori, why didn't you say something about this sooner?"

"I didn't think it was important."

"Didn't think it was important?" His voice rose, and he struggled to bring it to a professional level, to rein in the old Blaylock temper that always seemed to be lurking in the wings. "Tori, how could it not be important when Shannon is missing?"

"I—"

"Who is this guy? Do you have his name? His e-mail address?"

"I don't know his full name," Tori said. "His first name is Alex. And I don't remember his e-mail address. I used Shannon's computer to write to him, and it was just the one time. But it worked. He finally left her alone."

Lucas slapped a hand to his forehead, knocking his hat askew. "*It worked?* It worked?" His voice rose again. "Tori, are you kidding me? Shannon is *missing.*"

"I know that!"

"Well, you're not acting like you know it. Damn it, Shannon could've given this guy her address for all you know. He could be the one who took her. And why in the world would he listen to you telling him to get lost when he didn't listen to Shannon?"

Lowering her eyes, Tori shrugged.

"Tell me everything you know about him...about his relationship with her."

She burst into tears. "Lucas, stop yelling at me. If I'd thought of it, I would've told you. He was just some guy on the Internet. I don't know anything about him, or his relationship—if that's what you can even call it—with Shannon. It's cyberspace. Alex could be anyone."

"Exactly." Lucas barely restrained himself from slamming his fist on his desk. He rose, pacing the floor, hands shoved in his hip pockets. "Did she visit any chat rooms with him? Talk to him on the phone?"

"I don't know," Tori said, still crying. "If I did, I'd tell you. You know I'd do anything to help Shannon and Miranda and Paige."

Lucas took a deep breath. "I know you would, Tori. But try to see this from my point of view. Damn!" He paced some more. He'd have to get Carrie to look into things more closely. See if she could come up with anything…maybe a chat room Shannon had visited or something.

"How serious was she with this guy?" he asked, sitting on the edge of his desk.

Tori sniffed and wiped her eyes with a tissue. "I don't know," she snapped. "She's not really all that close with me. She just didn't want Miranda to find out, because she was embarrassed it had happened. So she asked me to help her instead. Really, Lucas, it's not like Shannon and I hang out together. Miranda's my best friend, not her."

Tori had a point. Still, Lucas couldn't let go of it. He kept worrying the information like a dog with a ham bone, taking down detailed notes. When he finally let Tori go, he picked up the phone and dialed Carrie. She was out, so he left her a voice mail.

An online romance. With God knows who.

He had to find Shannon.

CHAPTER ELEVEN

MIRANDA STOPPED AT THE grocery store on her way home from her mom's on Thursday. In the three days since she'd made love to Lucas, she'd lived in a cloud of confusion.

Made love. That wasn't really even an apt description of what had taken place between them. Hot sex was more like it. There'd been nothing tender about it, and she'd tried to avoid Lucas until she could clear her head.

She was surprised to see him approaching her in the produce aisle. She'd never expected to find him here. He strode toward her with purpose, looking solemn. Miranda braced herself for whatever he had to say.

"Can I talk to you for a minute?"

She shrugged. "Sure. What's up?"

He lowered his voice. "We found something odd on Shannon's computer. Can we meet someplace more private?"

Miranda swallowed, her mind still on the other night. "Of course. Do I need to leave these?" She indicated her groceries.

He shook his head. "Go ahead and check out. I'll meet you at my place."

"Your place? You mean your office?"

"No. I'd like to keep this quiet for now. I need to run home anyway. I've—uh—got a sick cat," he added sheepishly. "It's an upper respiratory thing. I need to give him a dose of antibiotics."

"Sure. Okay." Again, she swallowed hard. She knew where it was, but she'd never been there. Not to his ranch, anyway. He'd lived in a smaller house on the edge of town when they'd been engaged.

"See you in a while, then." He turned and started to walk away, only to pull up short as he passed Kyle Miller.

"Hey, Lucas," Kyle said. "Hi, Miranda."

"Hello, Kyle. How's it going?" Small talk. The last thing she wanted at the moment.

"Actually, I was on my way to your place. I thought I'd stop in here and get some doughnuts first, and I saw your truck." As Lucas must have. "What's your favorite?"

"Actually," Lucas said, "Miranda was on her way to my house." He stared the guy down, and Miranda fought the urge to kick him.

"Thank you anyway, Kyle," she said. "Maybe another time?"

"Yeah, sure," he said, giving Lucas a dirty look. "Guess I'll see you later, then."

"Sure, Kyle." She waited until he was out of ear-shot. "Lucas, was that necessary?"

"What?"

She crossed her arms. "You remember what we talked about before?"

He grimaced. "I know. It's just…"

She waited. "Just what?"

"I don't like him looking at you like a piece of meat."

Miranda's jaw dropped, but Lucas was already leaving. "See you in a few."

A piece of meat? He had to be kidding. As if he had anything to say about who she did or didn't see, anyway.

One thing was for sure. She planned to have a talk with Lucas once she found out what he wanted.

MIRANDA PULLED HER TRUCK to a halt at the edge of Lucas's property, all shaky inside. She felt like a kid on a first date. Only this wasn't a date, this was serious. Taking a deep breath, she turned into the driveway.

The ranch house was beautiful. Pine logs had been carefully overlapped, making it look like something out of a home builder's magazine. The roof was shingled in a warm shade of red and the porch wrapped around the front and one side, the log railing varnished to a shine. A huge serviceberry shrub stood centered in front, and along the nearby board fence, dividing the yard from the pasture, grew a row of ponderosa pines.

Two rocking chairs sat invitingly on the porch, a pair of mud-encrusted cowboy boots between them. One boot was tipped over, and a snow-white kitten poked its head out from inside. Nearby, on a cushioned bench, lay a huge gray tomcat, and on the steps sat an orange tabby. Miranda knew Lucas had liked cats when they were kids, but was surprised he owned more than one.

"Hey, kitties," she said as she climbed the steps. For a moment, the cats distracted her from the reason for her visit. But the minute Lucas opened the front door, her trepidation was back tenfold.

"Come on in," he said, motioning her into the living room. The white kitten took advantage of the opportunity to dart inside and disappear up a flight of oak stairs.

Miranda couldn't help checking out the room. Like the outside, the house inside was neat, well organized. It was built loft-style, with exposed wooden beams on the twelve-foot ceiling. A sectional sofa upholstered in dark leather took up most of the far corner. It bore the marks of cat claws, and was covered with a couple of matching afghans in a Navaho pattern. Plants hung everywhere, and Miranda wondered how Lucas kept the cats from getting into them.

"Have a seat." He indicated the sofa as he sat on one section of it.

Miranda settled a few cushions away…safety in distance. "So, what's up?" she asked, hoping it wasn't bad news.

"I didn't really want anyone at the county hearing about this right now," Lucas said. "Only Garrett knows." He hesitated. "Carrie Hopkins, over at the DA's office, took a closer look at Shannon's computer for me."

"And?" Miranda held her breath.

"There was an e-mail from Tori on it." He handed Miranda a piece of paper. She quickly scanned it, then felt as if she'd fallen down the rabbit hole. "I don't understand. Why would Shannon turn to Tori?"

"That's what I'd like you to find out, if you can. I talked to Tori this morning and she was pretty evasive. I thought maybe you could meet with her, then get back to me."

"Of course."

"Keep this under your hat for now, will you? If you tell your mom, she'll tell Fae and Mae, and the whole town will know about it. We always like to hold something back in a criminal investigation that only the perpetrator would know about. The guy Shannon's been communicating with could be anyone."

"Oh, man," Miranda said, feeling light-headed, thinking of the motorcycle in Silver Creek. "This is so not like her. What in thunder was she thinking?" Then something occurred to her. "Do you think one of those phone numbers on her cell bill could be to him?"

"I'm checking it out, believe me. Will you talk to Tori as soon as possible?"

"Of course. Right away." Miranda stood. "I'm not sure what her work schedule is today, but I'll stop by the diner, and if she's not there, I'll call her."

"Good enough."

She turned to leave, but he stopped her. "Miranda." She waited. "About the other night…"

"Forget it," she said. "We did something in the heat of the moment. That's all."

He nodded. "All right. Just as long as you're okay with it."

"No problem. See you later."

In her truck, she began to tremble as her thoughts and emotions whirled. No problem…hardly. Sleeping with Lucas had been the biggest mistake she'd made, next to getting engaged to him. He'd broken her heart once.

She wasn't about to let him do it again.

At the Truck Inn, Miranda pulled into the parking lot, but didn't see Tori's car. She dialed her cell number, and her friend answered on the second ring.

"Hey, kiddo, what's up?"

"I need to talk to you about something," Miranda said. "Have you got time?"

"Yeah, I don't have to work until my shift at the Spur tonight. Is something wrong?"

"I'm not sure yet. You at home?"

"Yeah. I think I know what this is about. Come on over."

Miranda flipped the phone shut, and drove to

Tori's house. Her friend lived in a cute mint-green house at the edge of town. She'd bought it from a musician whose band often played at the Silver Spur. He'd sold it when he'd gotten married.

She was waiting on the porch in a patio chair. "Want a Coke?" she asked.

Miranda shook her head. She sat in the chair next to Tori's. "I talked to Lucas today. He told me about the e-mail."

Her friend worked hard to keep her expression blank. "What e-mail?"

"The one Shannon wrote to you, thanking you for helping her dump her supposed Internet boyfriend. Tori, you and I both know Shannon would never date some guy she 'met' online. That's just not like her."

"Well, she did," Tori insisted. But she looked away and shifted uncomfortably in her chair.

"Why would she confide in you and not me?"

Tori shrugged. "Didn't Lucas tell you? I think she was embarrassed."

"And why is that?"

"Like I told Lucas, she made a big mistake in hooking up with this guy. He turned out to be a real jerk."

But Tori still wouldn't meet her gaze, and Miranda had known her long enough to be sure her friend was lying. Why, she had no idea.

"Why didn't you tell Lucas about this first thing? If

what you're saying is true, then how do we know this creep doesn't have something to do with Shannon's disappearance?"

"I doubt that."

Miranda laughed without humor. "You doubt it? What—suddenly you're a cop?"

"No," Tori said defensively. "But I'm sure if anything seriously threatening was going on, Shannon would've told me. Trust me."

"I want to," Miranda said. "But how can I when you held this information back? Tori, you had no right."

Her friend's face screwed up into a grimace of sorrow and regret. "I'm sorry, Miranda. I already apologized to Lucas. It's just that I really don't know much of anything about it."

"What exactly did you do to get rid of this guy?"

"I told him to back off—Lucas already knows all this."

"Yeah, well, *I* want to hear it. What would make this guy scared enough of you to leave Shannon alone, when he wasn't listening to her?"

"I threatened him," Tori said. "I told him Fae and Mae and I would throw him into a mud hole and then stomp it dry if he didn't stop bothering Shannon. That's it, Miranda, I swear."

Miranda studied her friend's expression. "You'd better not be lying to me, Tori. Shannon's life could be on the line."

Tori huffed a breath out between her pursed lips.

"As if I don't know that? Miranda, do you honestly think I would ever do anything to harm your sister?"

Miranda sighed. "No, of course not."

"All right then. Like I said, you'll just have to trust me on this one."

Silence stretched between them. She supposed Tori was right. At any rate, it seemed she had little choice. "Fine."

Tori stood and gave her a hug. "Now what say we order a pizza?"

Miranda wasn't really hungry, but she didn't have the heart to say no. She could see by her friend's red-rimmed eyes that she'd been crying. Miranda could just imagine how Lucas must've raked her over the coals.

After all, he did have the Blaylock temper. But he knew when enough was enough. Miranda wished she could say the same for his brother. Or his father, who was in prison for manslaughter after killing a man in a bar fight.

"Supersupreme with extra cheese?" Miranda asked.

Tori grinned. "I wouldn't have it any other way."

KYLE SHOWED UP AT Miranda's the next morning. He had Blackhawk with him, and was dressed sharply in Wrangler jeans, boots and a dark blue T-shirt that read *CSI: Las Vegas.*

"Hey, Kyle," Miranda said in greeting. "People are bound to believe that shirt is genuine with that big ole dog tagging along." She smiled, and he chuckled.

"Good point. But maybe that's not such a bad thing. Any news?"

It was on the tip of her tongue to mention the e-mail. "Nothing solid. But I'm not giving up."

"That's the spirit. I thought I'd come by and see if you want to go out this morning." He held up a paper sack. "I brought those doughnuts."

"How sweet. Thanks, Kyle."

After a doughnut and a cup of coffee, they set out on horseback, with Kyle dismounting every so often to search on foot with Blackhawk while the horses took a breather. As she watched him work the dog, Miranda thought back to the couple of times they'd gone out in high school, and she realized something. Ever since Lucas had humiliated her, she'd pretty much kept to herself, avoiding men. Was that what she really wanted? To be alone for the rest of her life?

Kyle was nice enough, and it was clear he was looking to start something with her. But Miranda just wasn't up for that. No, she didn't want to be alone forever, but Kyle wasn't the guy for her. While she appreciated his help, she couldn't go out with him, and hoped he wouldn't ask.

She had been dividing her time between her own place and the Rocking W. She was surprised Kyle had even caught her at home, since she usually spent mornings with her mom. She said as much to him when he returned to the horses.

"Actually, I stopped by your mom's place first,"

he admitted, a boyish flush creeping over his face. "I gave her a couple of doughnuts, but I don't think she ate them. She sure looks worn-out."

"I know." Miranda picked a burr from Ranger's mane and tossed it away.

If Shannon wasn't found soon, it might be best for Paige to come stay with her, she mused. That would certainly be easier on Miranda herself, not having to run back and forth between the two ranches. Chet and Sam would take care of the horses at the Rocking W, as well as running the stables, seeing to the customers' needs.

Besides, Paige didn't need constant reminders of her daughter's disappearance that came in the form of curious people arriving at the ranch not so much to ride, but to see where the "incident" had taken place.

Kyle left just before lunchtime, but not before asking Miranda if she'd like to go out for a bite to eat. She politely declined, hoping he would take the hint that she wasn't interested in him that way.

But to her chagrin, he returned that afternoon, and by the time she was able to politely ease him into going home, she was worn-out. After a shower and a light supper of chicken salad, she picked up the phone and called Tori. Her friend had every other Friday evening off, and it had been awhile since they'd gone to the movies. Miranda could use the distraction.

"Hey," she said when Tori answered. "You feel like taking in a movie? The new thriller is playing tonight."

"I'm not feeling real well this evening," her friend replied. "I think I'm coming down with a summer flu bug or something." She coughed. "Maybe it's just allergies."

"Bummer. Well, I guess you don't want to take a chance. Get some rest. It's no wonder you're sick, working two jobs all the time."

"You're one to talk, buddy. You've been under so much stress... Well, I don't need to tell you that. Why don't you get some rest, too?"

"I don't know," Miranda said. "I'm tired, but I don't really feel like staying home. I think I might just take in a movie by myself." If nothing else, it would give her time to think.

Miranda chose to go to the late show. It was normally less crowded. She drove down Main Street and came to the sole four-way stop in town.

And did a double take.

Tori had just driven past in her bright red Saturn, heading toward the highway. *What the hell?* Miranda drove on through the intersection, then flipped around in a U-turn and followed.

Before she'd driven even a block through the four-block town, her cell phone rang. "Damn it!" Miranda fumbled for it. She hated talking while driving. But when she checked the ID, she saw it was her mom's number.

"Mom?"

"Miranda, it's Sam. Get out here quick. Your mother collapsed in the bathroom. I've called 911."

Miranda sucked in her breath. "Is she okay? What happened?"

"I don't know. Chet had talked her into a card game, but when we knocked on the door, no one answered. We got worried and went on in, and that's when we found her. She woke right up, but she looks awful."

"I'm on my way." Miranda snapped the phone shut and stepped hard on the accelerator.

The drive to the Rocking W seemed endless. Her hands shook on the steering wheel. *No.* Not her mother. Miranda couldn't lose her, too. It was only as the thought registered that she realized she'd lost hope of finding Shannon alive. She'd been missing for a week now. What were the odds she'd ever come home? Miranda watched true crime shows. She knew the statistics.

By the time she arrived, Paige was already on a stretcher, and the paramedics were preparing to load her into the ambulance.

"Mom." Miranda rushed forward and took her mother's hand. "Are you all right?" She looked at one of the medics. "What's wrong with her?"

"Probably dehydration and lack of sleep. I'm sure she'll be fine, but we want to take her in to the hospital just to be on the safe side. You can follow along or ride with her."

She might need her truck, Miranda realized. "I'll follow."

The medic nodded, then helped her partner ready Paige.

"I'm here, Mom. It's going to be okay." Miranda bit her lip. She'd never seen her mom look so sick, so pale. Her eyes were closed, and she looked as if she'd aged ten years overnight. Miranda stepped back out of the way so the paramedics could do their job.

Paige moaned as they loaded her into the ambulance.

"Shannon," she called. "Where's Shannon?"

Heart breaking, Miranda got back in her truck and followed the orange-and-white emergency vehicle.

Its red, flashing lights cast an eerie glow on the dark road as they sped toward town.

CHAPTER TWELVE

PAIGE'S POOR CONDITION did indeed turn out to be dehydration, coupled with stress and lack of sleep. The emergency room doctor looked her over and instructed the nurses to prep her with an IV. She would be spending the night in the hospital as a precautionary measure.

Relieved, Miranda collapsed in a chair beside her mom's gurney. "You scared me," she said, grasping her hand. "As soon as you get out of this place, I'm taking you home with me."

"I'm fine," Paige insisted. "I don't need to stay here, and I don't need a babysitter."

"Fine?" Miranda shook her head. "I'd hardly call this fine, Mom. You're more mule-headed than me and Shannon put together." As soon as the words were out, she regretted bringing up her sister's name. But it wasn't as if Paige would simply forget about Shannon, just because Miranda didn't talk about her.

"Darn straight," Paige said. "Where do you think you girls get it from?"

Miranda couldn't help but chuckle. "What am I going to do with you?"

The nurse came in a short time later and gave Paige a sedative so she could sleep. Miranda kissed her mom on the cheek, then went outside to use her cell phone. She dialed Tori's number, but got her voice mail. She also tried her home phone, but her friend didn't answer there, either. Maybe she'd been called in to work, after all. Miranda dialed the diner first.

Mae answered, and Miranda told her what had happened.

"Lordy, honey. That's awful! But Tori's not here. She's off tonight, and as far as I know, she didn't have to work at the Spur."

"That's what I thought. Well, just have her phone me if you see her."

"Will do. And you give your mamma my best. Tell her to call if she needs anything."

Miranda hung up and dialed the Silver Spur, but had no luck there, either. Just then, her phone beeped, displaying Tori's cell number.

"Tori, where are you?" she said as soon as she picked up. "I've been trying to get hold of you."

"I got your message. Your mom's in the hospital? What happened?"

Miranda told her. Then she said, "I saw you driving down Main Street. I thought you were sick."

"Well, I was, but then I started feeling better."

"Where were you going?" Miranda knew she was

being nosy, but there was something too odd about Tori's behavior to ignore.

"Nowhere special," Tori said. "I just needed some air."

Air? "Tori, is everything okay?"

"Sure. Why do you ask?"

"You're acting weird. You're worrying me."

"Well, don't be worried," she said. "Just take care of your mom. I have to cover someone else's shift at the Spur tonight, as it turns out, but tell your mother I'll come out to the ranch to see her tomorrow."

"All right," Miranda said. "See you then."

Before she could go back inside, Lucas pulled into the parking lot. He left the Blazer and walked her way.

"How's your mom?"

"She's resting."

"I heard the call over the radio." He leaned against a brick pillar near the hospital entrance. "She's going to have to start taking better care of herself."

"Tell me about it. I'm going to have her come stay at my place for a while. That way I can keep a closer eye on her."

He nodded. "Not a bad idea."

Miranda stifled a yawn.

"Looks like you could use some rest yourself."

"I suppose." Just then a breeze kicked up, and she could smell the scent of Lucas's cologne. All sage and leather and totally him. Scent was supposed to be the strongest memory trigger, and Miranda would agree. Obviously, Lucas's taste in cologne hadn't changed much. She easily recognized the brand he wore, and just as easily, memories came back to her of the two of them in the moonlight...

"Miranda."

"Hmm? Oh, sorry. I just zoned out."

"I'd say so." He grinned.

Stop it. She had to quit thinking about Lucas.

"Want to see if they've got any coffee worth drinking in this place?" he asked.

"Sure." She followed him inside, to an area where vending machines stood clustered in an L-shape. "Lucas, something strange happened tonight. At least, I think it was strange."

"Oh?" He stood back and listened while they drank the bitter brew out of the machine. She explained what had happened with Tori.

He frowned. "I think I'll have another talk with her tomorrow."

Miranda felt like a traitor. "I hate to rat out my best friend. But Tori's not acting like herself."

"I'll check it out. Now, let's go see your mom."

The hospital checked Paige out at eight-thirty the next morning and, over her protests, Miranda drove her back to Bush Creek.

"This isn't necessary," her mother grumbled. "And if you're going to take me home to babysit me like some child, at least let me pack a bag with some of my stuff."

"I already did that," Miranda said, "last night. It's

just for a while, Mom. Until you catch up on your rest. Chet and Sam have got the stables under control."

"You could use a rest yourself," Paige said.

"You're right. I guess neither of us will do Shannon any good if we don't take care of ourselves."

Paige sighed. "True."

She looked so forlorn, Miranda wanted to do something to boost her spirits. As they went inside the house, she said, "Hey, let's pop some corn and watch a movie. What do you say?"

"That sounds pretty good." Paige smiled.

"All right, then." Miranda turned to go to the kitchen.

"Miranda."

"Hmm?"

Paige reached for her hand. "Thanks for looking out for me. I love you."

Miranda smiled and gave her a hug. "I love you, too."

LUCAS HAD MADE ARRANGEMENTS for Tori to meet him at his office that morning. She showed up a little past their appointment time, looking as if she hadn't slept well. She dropped into the chair in front of his desk.

"Thanks for coming in," he said.

"No problem. What can I do for you, Sheriff?"

"Well, I'm hoping you can answer a few questions." He purposely took his time, wanting to put her on edge to see if she would react nervously. Idly, he stacked some papers, then looked her in the eye. "Miranda says you told her you were sick last night, but then she saw you driving through town a short time later. Is that right?"

"Yeah, so? I felt better and decided to go for a drive. Is that a crime?"

"Why didn't you head over to Miranda's?"

She shrugged. "I figured she'd gone to the movies without me."

"Why not join her there?"

"It was halfway into the picture. I hate missing the beginning."

He leaned back in his chair, making a teepee of his fingers. "I see. Where did you go driving?"

Tori's face reddened. "Around. Just cruisin'."

"Uh-huh. Do you usually go cruising after you've felt sick?"

"Is there a point to this?" Tori asked, voice rising. "I don't usually *feel* sick."

"Just wondering if everything's okay with you. Miranda was worried that you were acting strangely."

"Well, I'm fine. She doesn't need to worry about me. She's got enough without adding to the list."

"I couldn't agree more. You haven't heard anything further from that guy on the Internet who was bothering Shannon, have you?"

"How could I? He doesn't know my name or my phone number, or even my e-mail address."

"Okay. Well, I don't have any other questions."

"So, I can go now?"

He nodded. "Just do me a favor, Tori. Be careful. You shouldn't be driving alone at night like that, especially now, given all that has happened."

"Have you gotten any word on the girl over in Cameron County?"

"Not yet. No one's come forward to claim the body."

Tori shuddered. "That's awful. Well, if that's it, then, I guess I'll see you later, Sheriff."

"Take care." Lucas watched her hurry outside and get in her car. She drove away a little too quickly, but he let it slide. He had other things on his mind.

Maybe it was time to pay another visit to Masterson. Maybe the man hadn't been convicted of the brutal rape of Jo Ella Jamison…yet. But Lucas knew enough about bad seeds, having grown up a Blaylock, to know he was guilty.

After all, Lucas was a Blaylock, like it or not.

MIRANDA WAS IN THE MIDDLE of a barrel racing lesson with Sissy Spangler when Tori pulled into her driveway. She looked grumpy, and Miranda was afraid she knew the reason why.

"Sissy, just keep working him on the pattern at a lope, and then walk a few circles around the outer edge of the arena. I'll be right back."

"Will do."

Miranda hurried over to Tori's car. Her friend had

parked some distance from the arena, and made no effort to get out.

"Hi," Miranda said. "What's happening?"

"Get in."

"What? Tori, I can't go anywhere. I'm giving Sissy Spangler a lesson—"

"We're not going anywhere. Just get in," Tori said firmly.

"All right." Miranda climbed into the passenger side of the Saturn. She closed the door. "What's up?"

"You know good and well what's up." Her friend looked hurt. "Why did you ask Lucas to grill me this morning?"

"Grill you? I hardly think—"

"Last time I checked, this was a free country. And a grown woman can go anywhere she pleases, day or night, without giving an explanation to anyone."

Miranda's jaw dropped, she was so taken aback by her friend's vehemence. Tori had the proverbial redhead's temper, but she'd never lost it with Miranda before. "Tori. What on earth is wrong?"

"You almost blew it for me, having me hauled in to Lucas's office like some naughty kid to the principal's. Miranda, I'm sorry I lied to you last night about not feeling well and not wanting to go to the movie, but there was a reason."

"Okay." Miranda stared at her, still taken aback.

Tori took a deep breath. "I'm seeing a married man."

Miranda couldn't have been more shocked if she

had announced she'd joined the Mormon Tabernacle Choir. "Oh, Tori. You're kidding, right?"

"No, I'm dead serious. And I want you to keep quiet about it. Don't even mention it to your mom, or she'll tell Aunt Fae and Aunt Mae, and I'll catch holy hell."

Miranda stared at her friend, unsure what to say. "All right. I promise not to tell anyone."

"Good. Last night I was on my way to see…well, to see my boyfriend. I don't want to name names. That's why I said no to a movie."

Miranda turned sideways in the bucket seat, tucking one foot up under her. She was hurt that her friend didn't trust her more than that. "I'm sorry, Tori. I didn't know, or I wouldn't have said anything."

"Well, now you know," Tori stated. A moment of silence passed. "You're not going to tell me it's wrong and that I'm out of my mind?"

"Hey, I'm in no position to sit in judgment." Miranda knew how badly a man could screw up a woman's head. Here she was, falling back in love with… Who was she to tell Tori who to go out with?

"I'm not delusional or anything," her friend murmured, lighting up a cigarette. "I'm not expecting him to leave his wife and marry me or anything like that." She puffed out a smoke ring.

"Just be careful, will you?"

"I will. I promise."

"Does he have any kids?"

"No questions, all right?"

"Okay." Miranda lifted her hands in a gesture of surrender. "Listen, I need to get back to Sissy. Call me later."

"Better yet, stop by the diner when you get done here. I've got an idea that might help us out. Now remember…not a word."

"Pick a lock," Miranda said, using their old childhood phrase as she twisted an imaginary key in an imaginary lock on her lips.

SHE ARRIVED AT THE Truck Inn between the breakfast and lunch shifts. Fae, Mae and Tori were hopping, trying to keep up with their customers. Miranda let out a groan as she entered the main room. Kyle was seated at the counter, sipping a cup of coffee and eating a sweet roll. While she was grateful for the guy's help, he was becoming annoying, sticking around so much.

Miranda pretended not to see him, and squeezed into a nearby seat between two truck drivers, who gave her appreciative smiles. She smiled, too, then buried her face in one of the laminated menus tucked between salt and pepper shakers. As if she didn't have the thing memorized.

"Miranda." Kyle stood at her elbow. "How are you doing today?"

Not so hot.

"As good as can be expected," she said.

"Come on back here, kiddo," Tori interrupted, rescuing her. "I've got something to talk to you about."

"Sure," Miranda said, rising from the high stool. "Nice seeing you, Kyle." She hurried after Tori, barely giving the guy a chance to answer.

Tori took her to a booth in the far corner where she and her aunts often did paperwork, or relaxed during their breaks. It was a given that the booth was the Lambert women's, and customers rarely sat there.

"So, what's up?" Miranda asked, once they were seated.

"I got to thinking," Tori murmured, keeping her voice low, "that some of the truckers who come through here are pretty rough characters. A lot of them have served jail time, or know someone who has." She looked around as though to make sure no one was listening. "I've been pumping them for information, seeing if they've heard anything or know anything, and it paid off." Her green eyes sparkled with satisfaction. "I found one who knows Lonnie Masterson—well, sort of."

"You didn't." A chill went up Miranda's spine.

"Not only that, this guy—Earl—has a friend who's still in prison. The friend heard Lonnie bragging about having sex with Jo Ella Jamison. Earl thinks Lonnie's lying about not having killed her. He also thinks Lonnie has some money stashed away from his last robbery."

"Oh my God. Then that could mean Lonnie might've had the money to hire someone on the outside to kill Shannon!" Miranda raked her hands through her hair.

"Simmer down, hon. I didn't call you over here to upset you. I just thought I should tell you before I tell Lucas."

"Earl knows Masterson…. He could be involved."

"I don't think Earl would be desperate enough to…take care of someone for Lonnie. He's really cleaned up his act."

"Anyway, it's all hypothetical. Lucas usually stops for coffee, but he didn't today, which means he'll likely come by for lunch."

"If I see him, I'll tell him."

Tori shrugged. "Whatever you want to do." She laid her hand on Miranda's. "Just watch your back. Not only because there's a killer out there, but because I don't want to see you get hurt. Lucas broke your heart once, and I'm afraid he'll do it again."

"I appreciate that, Tori, but you don't have to worry. Lucas and I aren't seeing each other."

"Okay," her friend said, in a tone that clearly let Miranda know she didn't believe her. "I'm dating my man with a grain of salt, believe you me. And most times a slice of lime and a shot of tequila." She slid from the booth. "See you later."

Miranda remained seated. Funny how easily

Tori could read her, and any situation involving her. That was just it. Miranda, too, was afraid Lucas would hurt her again.

CHAPTER THIRTEEN

WHEN MIRANDA GOT HOME, she found Paige's truck in the yard. How had it gotten there? But before she could storm inside and give her mother a butt chewing, a note taped to the mailbox caught Miranda's eye. Thinking it was from her mom, she snatched it off. The paper was damp, so it must've been outside since before the sun had risen that morning. How had she missed it?

Miranda frowned, then unfolded it and read: "You'd better leave things well enough alone, or you won't like the consequences."

She shivered. The note was made up of letters cut from newspapers and magazines, then glued to the plain white sheet. Like something on a TV show.

Realizing she shouldn't be handling the paper, Miranda held it gingerly by one corner and went inside the house, where she put it in an envelope. "Mom!" she called. "Where are you?"

No answer. Miranda made her way down the hall and found Paige sleeping in the guest room. The doctor had told them it would take her awhile to sleep off the sedatives he'd given her, plus he'd prescribed some Xanax to take as needed, to help relieve her stress and panic attacks.

Quietly closing the guest room door, Miranda went to the living room and dialed the sheriff's office. Within a short while, Lucas arrived. She gave him the envelope, and with a pair of tweezers, he carefully extracted the note.

"Who do you think did it?" Miranda asked.

"Could be anyone. It might be genuine, or it might be a prank. You'd be surprised at the nuts who come out of the woodwork when a crime is committed. The best thing to do is take it in to dust for prints." He'd already had Garrett and Frank collect fingerprints from Miranda, Paige, Chet and Sam for process of elimination.

"How soon will you know anything?"

"Well, it's not like you see on television. I can dust the note right away, but it'll take time to run the prints."

She nodded.

"Did you happen to stop by the diner and talk to Tori just now?"

"No, why?"

"She found something out." Miranda told him about Earl the truck driver and his connections to Lonnie Masterson.

Lucas pursed his lips. "You two need to step back from this. Let me handle it." He tapped her nose with his forefinger. "You're going to get into trouble and wind up hurt."

For a moment she stood there, staring at him. How long had it been since he'd tapped her on the nose that way, a gesture she'd once found endearing? "I'm not a child, Lucas, and neither is Tori."

He grumbled something, then took out his notepad and scribbled in it. "Guess I'd better go over to the diner and get this firsthand from Tori." He paused. "How's your mother doing, by the way?"

"Glad to be out of the hospital, but she wants to go home. I practically had to sit on her to get her to agree to stay with me for a while."

He smiled.

"Shannon's going to be proud of you when she comes home."

"Do you really believe that—that she's going to come home?" He didn't answer right away, and Miranda added, "Tell me the truth, Lucas."

He shuffled his feet on the porch boards. "I'm not giving up. Shannon could still be out there, alive."

Held against her will by some…

Better than being dead.

"Have they identified that woman over in Cameron County yet?"

Lucas shook his head. "Hopefully, someone will come forward soon."

"That's awful." Miranda became lost in thought about the way they'd all been frantically searching for Shannon, while another woman lay in a morgue, with no one at all, apparently, looking for her.

"Seems like you've had Kyle out there searching most every day," Lucas stated.

"Lucas," Miranda said, staring at him, "I can't believe you're still dwelling on this."

"On what?" he asked defensively.

"On Kyle."

He scowled. "It's just that I don't trust his motive in being at your ranch, or the Rocking W, every minute of the day."

"He's not here every minute. Lucas, what is wrong with you?"

"Nothing's wrong with me. I'm just seeing things a lot more clearly than you are."

"Oh, and what exactly are you seeing?" She folded her arms in front of her chest.

"That Kyle is exactly the kind of man you need."

"Excuse me?"

"Sure. He's a single dad, looking to round out his family. His kid's really cute, by the way. I met him the other day in the grocery store with his mom. And you— You've got your barrel racing students. You're great with kids and horses. Kyle's good with kids and dogs. Hell, you're practically already the Brady Bunch."

Miranda wanted to shake him. "I'm only going to say this one more time. Kyle and I are just friends. I do not *need* a man in my life. I'm perfectly happy with things the way they are. But whether or not I *want* a man—any man—in my life is my business and my business only. You got that?"

"Yes, ma'am." He smirked. "But I think the cow-girl doth protest too much."

"Do you want me to call my dogs?"

"Are you threatening an officer of the law? Be-cause I could handcuff you and run you in for that."

If she didn't know better, Miranda would think he was trying not to smile.

"Tell your mother I hope she gets to feeling better real soon."

With that, he tipped his cowboy hat and left Mi-randa standing there with her heart racing, and her mind going places it shouldn't.

LUCAS DROVE BACK TO THE office, his mind not at all where it should be. He wished things could've been different. Why did he have to be the son of a man who was utterly worthless?

Back at his office, Lucas checked in with Frank and Mac, who were on duty for swing shift.

"State police got back the lab results on the DNA for that blood you found on the rocks near the Rocking W," Frank said, "and from Shannon's saddle."

"And?"

"It's Shannon's all right," he said solemnly.

"Well, I guess we figured that." Lucas sighed. "Thanks for letting me know, Frank." He went to his desk and looked over the report, anyway. The state police had sent in strands from Shannon's hairbrush for a mitochondrial DNA test, and Lucas had pulled some strings, with a guy at the lab who owed him a favor, to put a rush on it. He'd needed to know for sure.

Lucas truly was beginning to think that Shannon was dead. Still, he wasn't about to give up. If there was even the smallest possibility that she could be alive, he'd bring her home.

And if she wasn't…well, he'd bring her home, anyway.

By Tuesday, Paige felt much better rested—and even had her appetite back. She insisted on driving home to the Rocking W in her own truck, which Chet and Sam had initially—against their will— driven out to Miranda's ranch, she'd later learned. Working the riding stable would keep her mother's mind busy as well as her hands.

To keep herself from feeling lonely the first night Paige was gone, Miranda called Tori to see if she could get away and go to the Silver Spur. Her friend had been working the diner that day, and assured Miranda she'd be off by six. By eight o'clock, the two of them walked into the place wearing their cowgirl best, which for Tori included a sparkly, silver Western shirt, big hoop earrings and white cowboy boots. Even on a weeknight, the honky-tonk was jumping.

"Are you sure you're not tired of this place?" Miranda asked, thinking—not for the first time—how dull her wardrobe was compared to her friend's. "We can go someplace else."

"Nah. This is close to home," Tori said. "Besides, it's nice to be on this side of the bar for once. So, do you want to sit at a table?"

"The bar. That way we'll likely see and talk to more people."

"Okay." Tori slid onto a bar stool, and Tina, her boss, walked over to serve them.

"What'll it be, dolls?" Blond and curvy, Tina was living proof that size twelve wasn't fat. She had a husky voice and thick, curly hair, and a way of winking at you that made you believe she was your best friend in the world. Tonight she wore her hair pulled into a twist at the back of her head, and hoop earrings like Tori's. Her long nails were painted copper, and she wore a frilly blouse, unbuttoned far enough to reveal ample cleavage.

"You can get me a kiss," one of the cowboys at the bar said, making smooching noises at Tina.

"Simmer down, cowboy," Tori said, elbowing him out of the way as she got comfortable on her stool. "Give me a Coors Light, Tina." She looked at Miranda. "Make that two."

"Coming right up. And you—" she pointed at the young cowboy "—mind your manners. I reserve the right not to serve drunks and fools."

"Aah, you're no fun." The cowboy teetered on his stool, but managed not to fall off.

Miranda chuckled.

"So," Tori said, once the two of them had their beers. "Where do you want to start?"

"How about that cute drunk sitting next to you?"

Tori cast a discreet glance in his direction. "You've got to be kidding. I know that guy—he's a regular. But he's three sheets to the wind."

"Exactly. There's nobody looser lipped than a drunk."

Tori raised an eyebrow. "I suppose you've got a point there." She swiveled her stool around, and Miranda slid off of hers, leaving her purse to hold her spot.

Beer in hand, she stepped up next to Tori's seat, beside the cowboy. "You look familiar," she said. "I know I've seen you in here before."

He drew back, looking her up and down. "Well, hello, pretty lady. Yeah, I come in here now and then. Ain't that right, Tori?"

"You bet, Jack. Now, then and whatever's in between."

He laughed and held out his hand. "Name's Jack McQuaid, darlin'." He took Miranda's hand, turned it over and planted a kiss on her knuckles. "What's yours, gorgeous?"

He looked barely old enough to drink. "Sally," Miranda said, causing Tori to choke.

"Well, Sally," Jack said, tipping his cowboy hat to the back of his head. "You must be tired, because you've been running through my mind all night long."

Oh, brother! "Is that right?" Miranda asked. "Well, maybe you can help me out with something."

"Anything you ask...it's yours. Including me." He spread both arms wide, and nearly fell off the stool this time. On the other side of him, a cowboy Miranda recognized guffawed.

"Jack, you're too drunk to sit up straight, much less do anything else." He shook hands with Miranda. "It's good to see you in here, Miranda." His family owned the local feed store. "I'm sure sorry to hear about your sister."

"Thanks, Darren. Listen, that's what I was going to ask Jack about. We think Shannon's disappearance has something to do with Lonnie Masterson, that guy who murdered Jo Ella Jamison. Do you know anything about him? Did you hear or see anything the night Jo Ella was murdered?"

"Ah, hell," Jack said, teetering upright on his stool once more. He grasped the edge of the bar for balance. "That no-good SOB. They ought to throw away the key, you ask me."

"You know him?" Miranda felt her hopes rising.

"No." Jack shook his head. "But anyone who would rape and kill a woman...well, let's put it this way. I'd like to have five minutes alone with him.

Wouldn't have to worry about no trial." He took a healthy swig from his longneck for emphasis.

"How about you, Darren?" Tori asked. "You were here that night, weren't you? Did you see anything?"

"Yeah, I was here. But all I saw was Jo Ella dancing with that feller. And your sister, she danced with him, too," Darren added.

Miranda shivered.

"I told all this to Sheriff Blaylock," Darren said. "Isn't he still investigating?"

"He is," Miranda said, "but Tori and I thought we'd just double-check with some of the folks who hang out here. Maybe see if Lucas missed anything."

"Aah…Lucas." Darren smiled. "So, you're still on a first name basis with the sheriff. I was only sixteen when he left you standing at the altar, but I still remember thinking what a fool he was. I would have thought you wouldn't even be speaking to him anymore."

Miranda groped for a reply, but Tori saved her the trouble.

"Lucas, Sheriff Blaylock…what's the difference, Darren? What we need to know is if you saw anything that night. How about you, Jack?"

"Aah, don't ask him." Darren waved his hand dismissively. "His brain's been pickled."

"Screw you, buddy," Jack said with a grin. "I did see something. I'm pretty sure I told the sheriff, but I'd had a few when he came around… No, I must've told him."

Miranda's pulse picked up speed. "What's that?"

"I saw Shannon leave the bar just after Jo Ella went out with that Masterson fella. Another guy started to go outside, too. But then he just looked out at the parking lot and ducked back inside."

Miranda exchanged a surprised glance with Tori. "Who was the other guy?" Tori asked.

"Don't know. I'd never seen him in here before."

"What did he look like?" Miranda pressed.

Jack shrugged. "Not as good as you," he said, his gaze a bit unfocused. "I don't know. Just some fella in a ball cap. Blue jeans. That's about all I remember. The only reason I remember that much is because he bumped into me as I was going to the men's room… Yeah, I'm sure I told Blaylock."

"So, he was going out the side exit," Tori said, again looking at Miranda. No one had known what door Jo Ella had used that night. Only that Shannon had gone outside and seen her struggling with Lonnie Masterson.

"That's right," Jack said, looking triumphant. "Only he came back in, like I said."

"You couldn't have told the sheriff," Tori said, "or we'd know this already."

"Told the sheriff what?"

Miranda jumped as Lucas tapped her on the shoulder. He held her purse up. "Do you always leave your stuff lying around where anyone can grab it?"

She snatched it from him. "How did you…? Never mind."

"What were you talking about?" Lucas's gaze pierced Jack's.

"Aah, um, nothing, Sheriff Blaylock," Jack stammered. "I was just saying as how I saw this one fella the night Jo Ella Jamison disappeared, but he didn't do nothing."

"No? Then why are you talking about him?"

"They asked me if I'd seen anything interesting that night." He gestured defensively at Tori and Miranda.

"So, did you?"

"Nah. Like I said, I just seen that one fella start to go out to the parking lot after Shannon Ward left. I only noticed it because I was going to the men's room."

"What'd he look like?"

Again, Jack gave his sketchy description.

"He didn't go outside?" Lucas asked.

Jack shook his head. "He started to, then he ducked back in and went back to the bar, I guess. I didn't see him anymore after that."

Lucas took a business card from his wallet. "Jack, you need to come see me tomorrow when you're sober." He slipped the card into the band of Jack's cowboy hat. "That's your reminder." Then he pointed a stern finger. "Don't let me see you out on the road driving tonight."

"No, sir," Jack said, clamping his palm against his chest in a gesture of innocence. "I'm the designated drunk." He chuckled. "And ole Darren here, he's driving."

"What've you had to drink, Darren?" Lucas asked.

"Just one beer, Sheriff. I swear. And that was earlier. I been suckin' down Cokes ever since. Ask Tina."

Tina had been off working the other end of the bar, but she'd come back in time to hear the tail end of the conversation. "What are you trying to do, Lucas, run off my customers?"

"Nope. Just trying to make sure they're alive to come back another day."

He turned to Tori and Miranda. "Might I have a word with you ladies? Someplace more quiet?"

"Sure," Tori said, sliding off her stool.

Miranda followed reluctantly. *What now?*

Lucas led them to a far corner near the restrooms. "What do you girls think you're doing?"

"What do you mean?" Miranda asked, crossing her ankles as she folded her arms and leaned against the wall.

"You know good and well what I mean." He stared her down, then glared at Tori. "Do you think this is a game?"

His words infuriated Miranda. "Not hardly, since it's my sister who is missing."

He winced. "I didn't mean it that way. I just don't want anything to happen to you, too. Or you either, Tori. You can't go around playing Nancy Drew."

"We weren't," Tori said. "We were only try-ing to—"

"What did Jack say?"

"Just what he told you," Miranda replied. "He'll fill you in tomorrow."

Lucas grunted. "If you're sure that's it…"

"I'm sure."

"All right, then." He hesitated. "I hate seeing either of you hanging out here at night."

"I work here," Tori said with a dry laugh.

"I realize that. If you want, I can escort you home."

"You're not serious." Miranda gaped at him. "Lucas, I appreciate your concern, but we're not chil-dren. I think we can take care of ourselves."

"I'm sure Jo Ella and Shannon thought the same thing," he said. "Keep your cell phones handy." With that, he turned and left.

"What was he doing here, anyway?" Miranda asked.

"He comes here on a regular basis, just looking things over," Tori said. "So do his deputies, especially after what happened."

Miranda pushed off from the wall with an angry bounce. "For Pete's sake, I feel like I've lost every-thing. My sister, my right to go where I please. How dare somebody do this to us?" She fought back tears. "How dare someone take my sister?"

Tori gave her a one-armed hug. "Hey, take it easy, kiddo. It'll be all right. Now what do you say we get out of here, and go have some pie and coffee? Aunt Fae made pecan, and coconut cream from scratch."

Miranda rubbed her eyes with her fingers. "You're trying to make me too heavy to ride my horse, aren't you?"

"Hey, whatever," Tori said with a grin. "Now come on."

Miranda made sure she had her cell in her hand as they left the Spur.

CHAPTER FOURTEEN

LUCAS CRUISED THE STREETS of Sage Bend, then drove past the Silver Spur, satisfied to see that Miranda's truck was no longer in the parking lot. He'd been keeping a close watch over the place ever since Jo Ella had been abducted, even though his deputies did regular patrol duty. He was one to do things himself.

By eleven o'clock, he could no longer resist the urge to drive by Miranda's place. From the end of the driveway he could see her truck beneath the yard light, and breathed a sigh of relief to know she'd gotten home safely. A shadow moved across the driveway—one of her dogs, the blue merle. The red one soon followed on its heels, and Lucas saw why.

Miranda was walking just ahead of them. He hadn't spotted her at first in the shadows cast from the barn. She was still wearing the clothes she'd had on at the Spur. The black jeans with a red blouse—her color. She wore her hair loose, and it fell down her back nearly to her waist. And she was going through the gate toward the creek.

Impulsively, Lucas pulled into the driveway, moving slowly to give her time to reach their spot.

It's not your spot anymore.

He parked, then walked as quietly as he could, knowing he risked being bitten—at the very least nipped—by those dang dogs. But she saw him before he got halfway across the yard, and she spoke to the dogs, commanding them to stay put.

He let out a breath and picked up his pace. "Long time no see."

"Lucas, what are you doing?"

He shrugged. "Just keeping an eye on your place."

"Trespassing?"

His face heated. "I'm only trying to make sure you're safe. Especially after the stunt you pulled tonight."

"I didn't pull a 'stunt.'" She put her hands on her hips as he slipped cautiously through the gate, keeping an eye on the dogs. They growled at him, but remained at Miranda's feet. "Do you realize you make my heart jump every time I see you like this?"

"Be still mine," he said with a grin, clamping both his hands over the left side of his chest.

Now it was her turn to blush. "I always think you've got news about Shannon."

"Damn, I'm sorry, Miranda. I didn't mean to do that." He just couldn't stop wanting to see her. Pretending he wasn't leery of the dogs, he walked by them and sat on the grass beside the creek.

He waited, holding his breath.

"You're starting to make a habit of this," she said, moving closer, but still standing.

"Am I?" Lucas rested his elbows on his knees. Thunder rumbled, and he noticed for the first time that clouds had blown in to cover the moon.

"At what exact point did you decide you were your brother and your dad all rolled into one? An hour before the wedding? How convenient."

He cast a sideways glance at her. "What did you want me to do, Miranda? Take the kids to visit Grandpa in the state pen? Explain to them why he lives behind bars?"

"Kids? You didn't give us a chance to get that far."

He stood. "You're right. Let's just leave the past in the past."

"I'm not the one who keeps coming onto your property."

Formally, he touched the brim of his hat. "'Scuse me, ma'am. I didn't mean to trespass." With that, he turned and walked away, hoping those damn dogs didn't heel him.

"Go on. Walk away," Miranda said. "You're real good at that."

He wanted to turn back and take her into his arms, kiss her senseless and tell her he loved her.

Instead, he went back to the Blazer and drove away.

HE WAS IN THE PERFECT mood to visit his brother. Even though Clint had done his share in helping to look for Shannon, Lucas heard rumors around town that his drinking had gone from bad to worse—so much for being on the wagon—and that he and Dena had been fighting a lot more lately. Would his brother ever learn?

The lights were on in most of the rooms of the house. Turning off his headlights, Lucas glided quietly down the gravel driveway and shut off the engine. He eased the SUV door shut and walked as carefully as he could around the side of the place. Already he could hear raised voices above the country music. He felt unexpectedly disappointed.

Lucas peered through the kitchen window, careful to stay back enough to not be seen.

He was just in time to see Clint backhand Dena.

That was it. Lucas's first instinct was to burst through the door and arrest his worthless brother. But common sense and law enforcement training told him he needed to follow procedure and call for backup.

In the Blazer, he radioed in. Garrett answered and promised he and Frank would be there right away. Lucas knew he should wait. But he couldn't leave Dena to get hit again. Lord knew, he was probably already too late for that. He went back and hammered on the door with his fist.

"Open up, Clint, or I swear I'll kick the door in!" It only took a heartbeat for Clint to yank it open.

"Well, well, if it isn't my big brother, come a callin'."
He gave Lucas a smirking grin. Clint held the door
wide. "Come on in, Lukie." Holding his temper in
check, Lucas stepped inside.

Dena sat at the table, unmoving. "Hi, Lucas. What
brings you out this way?"

"Thought I'd stop by and say hello," he told them.
"And here I am, just in time to witness that backhand
you gave your wife, Clint. What is wrong with you?"

"What goes on between me and Dena is our
business," Clint said, slurring his words.

"Well, it's my business now." Hearing sirens out
on the dirt road, Lucas stepped closer to his brother.
"Put your hands up where I can see 'em."

Clint gave him a dirty look, but complied, and as
Lucas patted him down, his anger suddenly vanished.
He knew it was the alcohol that made his brother
behave the way he did. They hadn't really had much
to do with each other in quite some time, but Lucas
recalled the days when they used to go fishing together, share a six-pack. A six-pack had turned into
a twelve-pack for Clint, then a case. And the gap between them had grown, until there seemed to be no
closeness left.

Lucas extracted a large, barely legal knife from
Clint's pocket. He laid it on the kitchen table amid
the playing cards and poker chips, then reached for
his handcuffs. "You're under arrest for domestic
violence. You have the right to remain silent—"

"Clint, don't arrest him," Dena said gently. "Please." She got up from the chair. "We were just arguing over the card game. It was nothing, really."

Lucas felt only pity as he stared at his sister-in-law. It was something he'd never understand— women who let men hit them. "Dena, it's the law. It's out of my hands." He pushed Clint toward the open door just as Garrett and Frank walked in.

"What's the problem here?" Garrett asked in a gruff voice.

"I witnessed Clint striking his wife in the face."

"No way," Clint retorted. "You weren't even here when—"

"When what, Clint?" Frank said.

"I can't frickin' believe this," Clint stormed. "My own brother, arresting me."

"Put a sock in it," Garrett said. "You brought this on yourself, Clint, same as usual."

"Why don't you come with me," Frank said to Dena. "Let's go into the living room and you can tell me what happened."

"She doesn't have anything to tell you," Clint said. "Do you, Dena?"

"I—"

"Don't let him bully you," Frank said, placing his hand lightly on her shoulder. "Come on. It'll be all right." He steered her from the room.

Lucas marched Clint out to the Blazer. "Watch

your head," he said, thrusting him into the backseat, wishing he could bash Clint's head against the door-jamb—knock some sense into him.

And suddenly, he saw the irony in that. Taking a deep breath, he pinned his brother with a hard gaze. "I'll be back."

"I'm not going anywhere," Clint grumbled.

And he wasn't. Normally, Lucas would've been worried about him bolting, even with the cuffs on. But the Blazer's back door handles were rigged to open only from the outside, and the front and rear seats were separated by a metal, mesh divider.

Back in the house, Frank was still questioning Dena. "So, what's going on?" Lucas asked.

"Apparently they got into it over a poker game," Frank said. "They had a couple of friends over, who left about twenty minutes ago. Anyway, Clint accused Dena of cheating."

"It's only because I was beating him," Dena said. "His ego couldn't take it. Clint thinks he's a card-sharp." She smirked. "Thinks he's better than those guys on TV even."

Lucas heard one of his nephews crying, from a room down the hall. Probably Cody, who was just three.

"Dena," Lucas said, "do you want Cody and Jason to grow up thinking this is the way to treat a woman?"

"I—" Her lip trembled. Abruptly, she turned to go to her sons, and disappeared down the hall.

FOR THE NEXT COUPLE OF days, all Miranda could think about, when she wasn't busy worrying over Shannon, was Lucas. The Fourth of July had come and gone, and she'd sat with Paige on the barn roof of the Rocking W, watching fireworks. But her heart wasn't in it.

She couldn't believe Lucas had actually left her house, only to arrest his brother. Clint had cooled his heels in a jail cell overnight. Had Lucas taken his anger at her out on Clint? Or had he simply wanted to prove to himself that he was nothing like the man? Would he ever believe it?

By Thursday, Shannon had been missing for almost two weeks. Neither the state police nor Lucas's team had found anything useful. The results of the fingerprints on the note Miranda had found taped to her mailbox—if there were any—were expected back soon.

Miranda drove to her mom's place just before supper with a bottle of wine in hand. She poured them each a glass, then dug one of Dena's casseroles out of the freezer to thaw in the microwave.

A short while later they sat in the living room, each balancing a plate of macaroni and hamburger, and thick slices of buttered garlic bread. One thing Paige did when she was nervous was bake, and Miranda bit into the bread with relish.

After a couple of glasses of wine, Paige said, "I think I'm going to head to bed. Why don't you stay?"

"I might just do that," Miranda replied. She'd had a little too much wine.

"Well, good night, then. Leave the dishes and I'll get them in the morning."

"All right."

The room seemed big and overly quiet once Paige left. Miranda wandered down the hall, but instead of going into her old room, she went into Shannon's. She turned on the light and was immediately overwhelmed by the familiar sights and scents. The double bed beneath the window, covered by a thick, navy-blue comforter with galloping horses decorating the fabric. Shannon's favorite stuffed animal—a ragged palomino horse—leaning against the pillows. Matching end tables with lamps made of twisted faux barbed wire.

The massive bookshelf on the far wall beside the closet. Some of Shannon's clothes draped on a chair; a pair of her old cowboy boots stuffed into the corner beside a wastebasket. On impulse, Miranda made her way to the trash can and looked inside, but it was empty.

Kicking off her own boots, Miranda sat on the edge of the bed and removed her jeans. She shut off the light and slid between the sheets. The moment her head hit the pillow, she could smell Shannon's favorite perfume. It was enough to undo her last resolve.

Miranda bit her lips to stop the burning tears. This was all so unfair. Shannon was a good person who'd never done a thing to harm anyone else.

Miranda stared at the ceiling until she finally fell asleep.

Lucas drove to Miranda's early Friday morning, after getting a call from Carrie Hopkins at the DA's office. What she had told him put a new light on things.

At any rate, Lucas wanted to smooth things over with Miranda, and was disappointed to find her truck wasn't in the driveway. Maybe she was at her mom's place.

He headed out to the Rocking W and was rewarded not only with the sight of her vehicle as he pulled up the long driveway, but Tori's car as well.

On the porch, Lucas knocked, and Paige opened the door. "Sheriff. Come on in." She held it open. "We were just sitting down to coffee. I'll get you a cup."

"Much obliged," he said, following her into the kitchen.

"Hey, Lucas," Tori said.

Miranda met his gaze, then looked away.

"How are you ladies holding up?" he asked.

"Hanging in," Miranda muttered. "Thanks, Mom," she added as Paige set a mug of steaming coffee in front of her.

"We're going to get through this," the older woman said, pouring Lucas an oversize mug.

"I'll just be glad when that stinking trial is over and Shannon is finally home," Tori said.

Lucas looked sharply at her. "What's the trial got to do with Shannon coming home?"

Her face turned red. "Nothing. I just meant I'll be glad when we find her, and the trial is over."

"That's not what you said." Lucas studied her, certain Tori was hiding something. "You said it as though, once the trial was over, Shannon would be home."

She gave a dry laugh, focusing on her coffee. "Don't be ridiculous. The trial's another week away, and Shannon's going to be found any day now."

But her expression didn't match her words.

"Lucas, what are you getting at?" Miranda demanded.

"I'll let you know when I'm sure," he said. "Tori, can I talk to you in the other room for a minute?"

She set her mug down, sloshing coffee over the rim, then quickly wiping it up with a napkin. "Sure." She made an effort to look carefree as she stood. "Whatever."

Lucas motioned her into the living room.

She sat on one end of the couch, and he took the chair right next to her. "Tori, if there's anything you know that you haven't already told me, you need to now." He pulled out his ace in the hole. "I had Carrie Hopkins, from the DA's office, go through Shannon's e-mails again. She searched through the trash can and pulled up all of the deleted files that had been dumped."

Tori's eyes widened.

"Nothing's ever really gone from your computer, if a person has the knowledge to find it again. I think you know what I'm about to say."

Tori merely shrugged.

"There were no e-mails from anyone named Alex,

or to anyone named Alex. In fact, there was nothing at all to any guy who'd supposedly been harassing Shannon. Do you want to tell me now what Shannon's e-mail to you meant—thanking you for helping her?"

Tori began to tremble. "Oh, Lucas, please don't be mad at me. I was only doing what I thought was best."

"Explain."

She took a deep breath. "Hang on a minute." She went to the kitchen and came back with her purse. She pulled out an envelope. "I think I know what's in this, but not for sure. Open it."

Lucas frowned and took the business-size envelope from her. Inside was a folded sheet of paper and several photographs. His blood turned to ice. In the letter, someone had threatened to kill Miranda and Paige if Shannon testified against Lonnie Masterson. As though to back up the threat, the two were photographed going about their daily business.

Someone had been watching Miranda—watching her mom....

"Miranda, get in here," Lucas called.

She hurried into the room, Paige on her heels. "What is it? What's wrong?"

He laid the letter and photos out on the coffee table, pulling a pen from his pocket. He used the capped tip of the pen to move the items around, spreading them out. "Don't touch these. Just look."

She did, and her face went pale. Paige let out a gasp.

"Where did you get these?" Lucas demanded.

"From Shannon," Tori answered. Tears filled her eyes. "She told me about the threats, but I didn't know what was in the envelope, Lucas, I swear. She just gave it to me and asked me to turn it over to you if anything happened to her."

"And you didn't consider her disappearance to be 'anything'?"

"Tori, *what* is going on?" Miranda looked from her to Lucas. "Lucas?"

Paige began to shake. "This isn't happening."

"Mom, calm down," Miranda said.

"To hell with that, I want my daughter." She slammed her fist on the table, making the centerpiece of dried flowers jump. "Who is *doing* this?"

"I don't know," Tori said. "But Shannon is all right."

Miranda sat next to her friend. "I want to believe that, too, but considering that letter and those photos—"

"No." Tori shook her head. "You don't understand. Shannon is fine, and I'm sure of it, because I know where she is."

Lucas bit back a curse.

Miranda stared blankly at Tori. "What?"

Tori gulped in air and started to cry. "I know where she is, because I helped her hide."

CHAPTER FIFTEEN

"WHAT DID YOU SAY?" Miranda could only continue to stare stupidly at her friend.

"Oh, crap." Tori raked her hands through her hair.

"Tori! What are you saying? Where's Shannon?"

"I can't tell you."

"What do you mean, you can't tell us?" Lucas demanded.

Miranda wasn't altogether sure her ears weren't playing tricks on her. "Are you serious?"

"Yes, I'm serious. Shannon's life is in danger, as you can see—" she gestured toward the letter and photos "—and so is yours and your mom's. Lucas, please try to understand." A look of misery contorted her face. "I really don't know where to begin."

"How about with how you came to have the note and photos?" Lucas said.

Miranda shook her head in disbelief. "Does this have anything to do with that guy she met online?"

"There wasn't any guy."

"*What?*" Miranda felt as if she was dreaming some horrible nightmare. She hoped she'd wake up soon.

"I just had to make up something on the spot to cover when you found that e-mail Shannon sent me, Lucas. Shannon was really thanking me for helping her with this whole mess…helping her find a safe way out of it. At least, I thought it was safe."

"Okay," Lucas said. "Start at the beginning."

Tori took a deep breath, but her voice was choked as she spoke. "I was the one who called Shannon the night before she disappeared. I used a disposable cell phone, so no one could trace it. Shannon just wanted me to check in one last time before…" Tori stopped and looked down.

"But why wouldn't Shannon show these to Lucas?" Miranda asked. Then it dawned on her. "Oh God. It's Lonnie Masterson who's threatening her, isn't it?"

"Yes. Shannon got those pictures and that note, and she freaked out. She didn't want you to know about it, and she was afraid to go to Lucas, so she contacted me. She didn't know who else to talk to. She was afraid if she testified at Lonnie's trial, his contacts on the outside would kill you and your mom. They told her not to go to the sheriff."

Miranda was stunned. "So she hid?"

"She thought if she went undercover until the trial was over, she wouldn't have to testify, and Lonnie would go free. Then he'd quit threatening all of you, and everything would go back to normal. Well, as normal as you can get with a murderer on the streets."

"You know that's not realistic," Lucas said.

"No, but it was the best plan Shannon could come up with under the circumstances. She just couldn't risk your lives."

"But if Shannon doesn't testify," Paige said, "she'll go to jail for ignoring the subpoena and not showing up for the trial."

"Better to be in jail than to have her sister and her mother dead."

Tori looked so solemn, it scared Miranda. She'd never seen her like this before. "I can't believe she'd do that.... I can't believe *you'd* do this to *me!* Lie to me. You're supposed to be my best friend."

"I *am* your best friend." Now Tori looked hurt. "Why do you think I did all of this? It's because I didn't want to see you dead, either!"

"Where is she?" Lucas asked.

Tori hung her head. "I can't tell you. Not until Masterson's trial is over."

"Tori…" He looked at her, exasperated.

"Wait a minute," Miranda said. "You helped us search the day she vanished. How could you have been in two places at once?"

"I didn't join the search until later."

"Tell me how you helped Shannon disappear," Lucas demanded.

"I can't give you any details." Tori looked miserable. "Lucas, please trust me on this. I don't want to put anyone's life in jeopardy."

"Well, that's exactly what you'll be doing if you

don't tell me everything, including where Shannon is. Look, Tori, just because she doesn't show up for the trial, there's no guarantee Masterson and his buddies won't go after her later. And you, too, and Miranda and Paige… Do you think their word means anything? You've got to tell me where she is."

"It wasn't supposed to happen this way," Tori sobbed. "Everything was supposed to work out so nobody got hurt."

"Tori," Miranda said, looking her right in the eyes. "Please."

Her friend slumped against the couch cushions. "She's at my grandpa's cabin."

Of course! Roy Lambert had an old hunting cabin up in the high country.

"With him in the nursing home, and me keeping the place up, we figured no one would think anything of it if they saw me coming and going."

She looked over at Miranda. "The night you asked me to the movies, Shannon was sick. I'd been up there earlier to check on her and take her a few groceries. She had a fever and a sore throat. I was delivering some cold medicine and aspirin when you spotted me."

"So you weren't…"

"No, I wasn't going to see anyone else. There's no married man." She scuffed her foot on the floor. "I've turned into such a liar."

Miranda let out a sigh of relief. "I knew you were better than that."

"What married man?" Lucas asked.

"I told Miranda—"

"Tori said—"

He held up his hand. "Never mind. We'll get this all down in a formal report later. Just tell me one thing, Tori. How did you get Shannon to the cabin in the first place?"

"I waited for her in Aunt Mae's truck up on an old logging road above the creek, about a mile from where you found her hair scrunchie. It's barely passable anymore, and we covered up our tire tracks with tree branches as we drove out. We had prearranged a time for me to be there. I took my four-wheeler with me, in the pickup bed. I drove Shannon up near the cabin, and dropped her off. She went in the rest of the way on the four-wheeler. That way she wouldn't be completely stranded."

"And what about the blood on the rock and on her saddle?"

"Shannon cut her palm with a pocket knife. She wanted you all to think she'd been hurt and kidnapped."

"I'm going to kill her," Paige said.

"She had to make it look believable. She'd ridden Poker hard enough to make him sweaty—she hated that part of it just as much as she hated deceiving you all."

"I checked the logging road," Lucas grumbled. "I didn't see your tracks."

"Like I said, we tried to hide them as best we could where we came out onto the main road."

"Well, apparently you succeeded," Paige snapped. "Tori, I'm mighty disappointed in you."

"All right, that'll do for now," Lucas said. "We need to get Shannon and bring her home." He took out his cell phone. "I'm calling dispatch to radio the state police."

"I'm so sorry," Tori repeated. "I know this has been really hard on you, Paige." She breathed in with a sob. "You have no idea how hard it was to keep lying to you. I feel just awful."

"They threatened me, too, you know," Miranda said.

"What?" Tori stared at her.

"I got a note taped to my mailbox, telling me to butt out. And someone shot at me and Lucas."

Tori cringed. "I did the note. And I also fired those shots to scare you and Lucas. I didn't want you to get hurt, so I tried to scare you away."

Miranda's jaw dropped. "You *shot* at us?"

"Not at you. Near you. I made sure I wasn't close enough to hit you." She lowered her gaze. "I got the idea the other night when you told me about your plans to ride out with Lucas. I drove up early that morning to a road the hunters use, in the general area where I thought you'd be. Then I hiked up to a point overlooking the trail and waited." She shrugged. "After I fired the shots, I hightailed it back to the Truck Inn while the two of you were pinned down, hiding in the rocks."

"You do realize that's called reckless endangerment?" Lucas said, closing his cell phone. "Tori, I'm afraid I have no choice but to write you up on that, as well as on lying to the police."

Tori looked so forlorn, it broke Miranda's heart. She knew her friend's intentions had been good.

"I didn't mean it," Tori said, tears sliding down her cheeks. "I was only trying to keep you all safe. I knew if you kept poking around, you'd find Shannon, and then Lonnie Masterson and his low-life, scumbag buddies would be all over you."

"Never mind, Tori," Miranda said. "Let's just go get Shannon." She let out a whoop.

"Hold up," Lucas said. "We're not going to do this again." He put his hand on Miranda's shoulder. "This time you really do need to stay put. I'm serious."

"Lucas." She gave him an exasperated look. Ignoring her, he used his cell to call Garrett and Mac.

"I want to see my daughter," Paige said stubbornly, as soon as he got off the phone.

"You will," Lucas said. "As soon as we get her, we'll bring her home. Now we're wasting time." Lucas tapped his cell phone. "I'll call you the minute we reach her. I promise."

Paige looked hesitant. "I don't want to get in the way," she said. "Cripes, this is hard." She clenched and unclenched her fists, pacing. "Oh, all right. Just hurry, Lucas. Please."

"Be careful," Miranda said with a sigh.

Lucas nodded, then hurried outside when Garrett and Mac pulled in. Mac went inside to question Tori, while Garrett left with Lucas.

"I don't think I can sit still that long," Paige said. She continued to pace the kitchen floor.

"I know I can't," Miranda declared. She reached for her keys. "I'm going up there."

"Miranda, you heard the sheriff."

"Yeah, I heard him. But my sister's been gone way too long. I'm not waiting another minute to see her."

"Be careful," Paige said, echoing Miranda's earlier sentiment to Lucas.

"You know I will." She hurried out to her truck and leaped into it, pushing the engine for all it was worth as she drove toward the cabin. Taking a shortcut, she managed to catch up with Lucas when she came back out on the main route a mile from the place.

She knew Lucas would be ready to curse when he spotted her behind him in his mirror. She didn't care. Nothing was going to stand between her and Shannon now. Miranda followed Lucas as he guided the Blazer up the narrow, twisting road.

She still found it hard to believe that Tori had lied to her all this time, even going so far as to tell such elaborate stories like seeing a married man. It hurt that her friend had betrayed her, even if Tori had thought her reasons justified it. But Miranda knew that if the shoe were on the other foot, she would do the same to protect Tori, Fae and Mae.

Miranda turned off onto a dirt road and parked as close to the small cabin as she could get, since the road ended several yards from the entrance. Lucas had already pulled over and stood waiting for her.

"Damn it, Miranda, don't you ever listen?"

"No." She gave him a challenging look. Then, pushing past him, she hurried toward the cabin.

She could hear Lucas on her heels. She ducked between towering pine trees and straight to the front door.

"Miranda, wait," Lucas called, just behind her.

He put his hand on her shoulder, but she shrugged out of his grasp and flung the door open.

"Shannon! It's me." She froze in her tracks as sunlight illuminated the room. "No."

Glass from a shattered window and broken dishes were scattered across the floor. A kitchen chair lay on its side, a carton of milk spilled next to it, still leaking a white, sticky pool across the hardwood floor.

There was no sign of Shannon.

LUCAS CURSED AS HE SURVEYED the room. Garrett paused at his elbow. "What's wrong? Oh hell."

"You need to go back to your truck," Lucas said to Miranda, knowing she wouldn't listen. "Go home."

Without a word, she turned and ran to her vehicle, and he stared after her openmouthed. Surely Miranda wouldn't comply this easily. Following, Lucas reached the open door of her truck just in time to hear her thanking Kyle Miller on her cell phone. He gritted his teeth. But then, calling Kyle out here might not be such a bad idea.

"Lucas," said Miranda, "please don't tell me to go home." Miranda shivered. "If anything happens to her, I'll never forgive myself. I should've thought to look in this cabin sooner, but I never dreamed Tori would betray me."

"She didn't really," Lucas said. "I'm not saying what she did was right, but her heart was in the right place."

"I know." Miranda pursed her lips. "But it's still a bitter pill to swallow."

Kyle, who'd been staying in town to be close at hand, arrived in short order.

Lucas supposed he had to admire the guy's attitude. The state police should have been here by now. Lucas didn't want to wait. "I'll lead the way once your dog picks up Shannon's scent," he said to Kyle.

"I'll need something for that," Kyle said. "I can start at the cabin."

"I have something here to get him on the right track," Miranda said. From the glove box of her truck, she took out a pair of leather gloves. "These are Shannon's. She left them in here the last time we were repairing fence line."

"Perfect." Kyle took the gloves and waved them under Blackhawk's nose, giving the dog encouragement and the command to go find. He let Blackhawk sniff a trail to the cabin, then back outside again.

The shepherd picked up on Shannon's scent leading away through the trees, and Lucas had to admire the dog's abilities yet again. He imagined it took a great deal of skill and patience to train and work with such an animal, and suddenly he felt annoyed at himself for having ever been jealous of Kyle. The man had been indispensable. Lucas set off right behind him.

Garrett had joined them, and he motioned for Miranda to go ahead of him. "I'll take up the rear," he said, "in case anyone backtracks on our tail."

They trekked along as silently as possible. Blackhawk led them through the trees to a narrow trail behind the cabin. And suddenly, a woman's muffled sobs carried to them on the early morning breeze. Before Lucas could react, Miranda sprang forward.

"Shannon!" she called. "Shannon, I'm here."

Cursing, Lucas drew his gun and hurried after her, Garrett beside him. He reached a bend in the trail just in time to see Miranda kneeling beside Shannon, who was bound and gagged. Tears streaked her dirty face, and she struggled to communicate as Miranda gathered her into a bear hug.

"Oh, Shannon. Oh, thank God." Miranda carefully removed the duct tape and wad of gauze from here sister's mouth. "Who did this to you?"

Shannon tried to answer, but only managed to cough and choke. Furious, Lucas holstered his weapon and began working to untie the ropes at her wrists while Garrett freed her ankles.

"Never mind," Lucas said, pulling out his pocket knife. "Let's just get you untied and out of here." He wanted to hurry—get everybody back to the cabin. Then he and Garrett would search the woods.

"He's right out there," Shannon finally managed to gasp. Terrified, she raised her arm to point at the trees. "He heard you coming and hid. He was going to kill me." She broke into sobs.

Lucas drew his gun once more, peering through the trees. "Wherever you are, come out. Now!"

Behind him, he heard Blackhawk bark. "He's spotted something," Kyle said. He hurried forward before Lucas could stop him, and the deafening crack of a gunshot fired at close range rang out.

"Get down!" Lucas commanded, pressing Miranda and Shannon to the ground. "Get behind that brush." He moved them behind him as fast as he was able. Pistol at the ready, he crept cautiously toward the trees where Kyle had disappeared.

"I've got your back," Garrett said, gripping his own gun.

As they drew closer to the pines and aspens, Lucas saw a man approaching Kyle, who was lying on the ground. Kyle dropped Blackhawk's leash and the dog lunged, grabbing the man's gun arm between his teeth. With a pull of his powerful jaws, he yanked it downward, causing him to drop the weapon. The guy half turned in the process of stumbling, and Lucas sucked in a startled breath.

Clint.

His own brother had shot Kyle.

Snarling nearly as loudly as the dog, Clint reached into his waistband with his left hand and pulled out a second pistol.

"Drop it!" Garrett shouted, coming up beside Lucas. "Now."

"So help me, Clint," Lucas said from between clenched teeth, "I won't hesitate to shoot you. Give me a reason." *Just one.*

Defiantly, Clint pointed the semiautomatic right at him, the twisted, angry look on his face more animal than human.

Lucas aimed and fired. At the same time, he felt something graze his shoulder.

Clint screamed and dropped the gun, grasping his wounded leg as Blackhawk bit and pulled on his arm. From the ground, Kyle called off his dog, and Lucas and Garrett quickly moved in to handcuff Clint. Lucas shoved his brother against some rocks, pushing his face into them.

"That's right," Clint taunted. "Go ahead and rough me up, Lukie." He laughed. "You can hide behind that badge of yours all you want, but you're still a Blaylock. This just proves nothing will ever change that."

"Keep your mouth shut," Lucas said. "You have the right to remain silent…" He recited the Miranda warnings. While Garrett patted Clint down to make sure he had no other weapons.

IT WAS ONLY WHEN paramedics started arriving on the scene that Lucas realized the extent of his wound.

"Lucas," Miranda said, hovering frantically between him and Shannon. "You're bleeding pretty badly." She tore off the sleeve of her shirt and pressed it against his shoulder.

Lucas winced. "It's just a flesh wound, ma'am," he said, feeling somewhat light-headed. "What about Kyle?"

"We've got him," one of the medics said. "We'll have you all out of here in no time."

Garrett pulled Clint to his feet, despite the leg wound and half dragged him down the trail toward the cabin. Two state policemen, looking huge and angry, arrived on the scene and hovered over Clint and Garrett. Lucas tried to wave the paramedics away, but Miranda told him to sit still.

"You listen about as well as I do," she said.

"Speaking of which," Lucas muttered, "I told you to stay home. Now go on and get out of here. Your family needs you." The medics had put Shannon on a stretcher and begun to take her down the trail, since the slope was too steep and the woods too thick for an ambulance. They would carry her to the road below the cabin.

"And I told you I wouldn't rest until my sister was safe," Miranda said. "And now she is."

"Then get out of here," he said. "I mean it, Miranda." Clint's words would not leave his mind.

You're still a Blaylock. "Your help is no longer needed or wanted. I never asked for it in the first place." He stared her down, steeling himself against the hurt that flashed in her eyes. Knowing it was all for the best.

Shannon was safe.

Now he and Miranda could go back to being strangers in a small town.

CHAPTER SIXTEEN

LUCAS'S WORDS CUT LIKE a knife, but Miranda refused to let her feelings show. Besides, she really did have her family to think of right now. She was overjoyed that Shannon was safe. Miranda was pretty sure her sister was more scared than hurt. She appeared to only have a few bumps and bruises, from what Miranda could see.

Their mother would likely have already heard the news of Shannon's rescue from Fae and Mae over the police scanner. Nevertheless, Miranda dug out her cell phone once she reached her truck. She followed the ambulance, glancing down at the device now and then, waiting for a better signal before she dialed her mom.

Paige informed her that she and Tori were already on their way to the hospital. "We'll meet you in the emergency room waiting area," she said. "I can't believe you found your sister." She choked up.

"Me, neither," Miranda said. "See you in a few." She snapped the cell phone shut. And then, as she thought about Tori, something dawned on her. Once everyone had arrived, Miranda made a beeline for

Mac in the hallway. He and the other deputies had come to the hospital to make sure Lucas was all right.

"Mac," she said, knowing it would likely be a while before the nurses would let her see Shannon, "I have a question for you."

"Shoot," he said, then grimaced. "Poor choice of words."

Miranda managed a smile. "Why didn't you arrest Tori when you took her statement? Is she in trouble for what she did?"

Mac shifted, placing one big hand on his utility belt. "I probably shouldn't be telling you this, but…" He looked at her pleading eyes. "Well, like Lucas said, she's likely to be charged with lying to the police. But try not to worry, Miranda. Tori didn't file a false police report, because she didn't file a report at all. She didn't kidnap your sister—Shannon was hiding of her own free will. And the last time I checked, there was nothing in the law books saying a friend can't supply another friend with groceries and a place to stay." He shrugged. "Plus she did turn over the evidence she had, even if it took her a while. But she and your sister will most definitely have to make restitution for the cost the county put out on all those search hours. Still, I doubt anyone's going to jail. I'd say even Tori is probably looking at probation and community service."

Miranda breathed a sigh of relief. "Thanks, Mac. I appreciate it."

"No problem, ma'am." He frowned. "I sure hope Lucas is all right."

"I'm pretty sure he is," she replied, denying the fear that gripped her. "I think the bullet just grazed his shoulder. I don't think it went straight in." If he'd taken a direct hit, then he must've been in too much shock for it to have registered. He'd been walking around just fine—lucid enough to tell her to leave.

But then, there was nothing new in that.

Miranda excused herself and hurried down the hall to the room where two nurses were working on her sister. One was taking her blood pressure, the other looking over the bruises that were beginning to blacken her wrists and ankles. The second nurse told Shannon a doctor would be in shortly.

The patient lay against a pillow on a hospital gurney, looking worn but happy. Paige hovered beside her, holding her hand.

"Am I dreaming?" Miranda asked.

"Come here and I'll pinch you," Shannon said. She held her arms out, and Miranda moved past the nurses to give her a hug.

Tears burned her eyes, but she blinked them back. No more crying. Shannon was home safe. But when she drew back, she saw that her sister, too, had tears on her cheeks.

Quickly, Shannon wiped them away. "It's so good to see you, Mia." She hadn't called her that in years.

"You, too." Miranda gave her sister a crooked

grin. "You had us all so worried," she said, cuffing her lightly on the shoulder. "Don't you ever pull a stunt like that again."

"No worries there. I'm so sorry."

"You've got some explaining to do, young lady," Paige said. "Just as soon as you're on your feet."

When Shannon reached for her hand again and gave it a squeeze, Paige turned Shannon's own hand palm up, exposing her self-inflicted, half-healed wound.

"That's a nasty cut. You'd better have these nurses look at it."

"They already have," Shannon said. She grimaced. "It keeps breaking open, but the doctor's going to fix me right up." She turned to Miranda. "Is Lucas okay?"

"He's wounded, but I don't think it's serious. I wanted to see you before I checked on him. It looks infected."

"Well, go on." Shannon shooed her away. "Check on that brave cowboy."

"All right. But we've got a lot of catching up to do."

"Miranda?"

She paused, looking back at her sister.

"You're brave, too. The bravest person I know."

Miranda felt her cheeks flush. "I'll be right back."

Her heart beating with trepidation, she headed to another group of exam rooms, searching for Lucas. She found him in short order.

But the moment she entered the room, one of the nurses tending to his wound looked up with a scowl.

"You can't come in here, miss. The doctor is on his way down to take care of this young man's injury."

"Just five minutes?"

The nurse pursed her lips. "Three. Starting now." She left the room after pulling a curtain partway around Lucas's gurney, separating him from the person coming into the next exam area.

"Hey, there," Miranda said, stepping up beside Lucas. She indicated the gauze-packed wound. "Does it hurt very much?"

He grunted. "I'll live."

"You'll never know how grateful I am to you for everything you did to help us bring Shannon home."

"You're welcome," he said. "Speaking of Shannon, what are you doing here with me? Your family needs you, not me. Go on, get out of here."

"You don't have to be so rude." Miranda scowled.

"I'm not. I'm just stating a fact." He stared at her, his gaze impersonal, almost cold.

She supposed it was only natural that he'd be cranky. After all, he'd just been shot, and he'd had to shoot his own brother.

"Okay, Mr. Grouchy. I've already used up two of the three minutes Nurse Ratchet gave me, anyway." Still, Miranda hesitated. It seemed wrong to just walk away and leave him. What would happen now? Would they see each other again? Or did he truly expect her to go back to the way things had been before Shannon's disappearance?

Miranda swallowed, finding a lump in her throat. If that's what he expected, he was a little too late. She'd never stop loving him.

"Take care of yourself, Lucas." Fighting the urge to reach out and clasp him in her arms, she turned and left the room.

MIRANDA DROVE HOME AN hour later, after promising her mom and sister she'd come straight to the Rocking W as soon as she took care of her animals. Shannon had been released, and was already on her way back with Paige.

Smudge and Tuck greeted Miranda as though she'd been gone a week. She ruffled their fur and took a minute to romp with them. She should be exhausted. Instead, she felt elated, in spite of Lucas's stinging dismissal. Shannon was home.

Once Miranda had everyone fed and watered, she packed an overnight bag, loaded a joyful Tuck and Smudge into the truck and drove to her mother's.

She found Shannon propped up on the couch in the living room, with Paige hovering over her, offering food and extra pillows.

"I can't believe you're finally home," Paige exclaimed. "By the way, Miranda, Lucas was released, too. But the stubborn fool went right back to work."

"Let me guess," she said with a smile. "You heard this through Fae and Mae."

Her mom chuckled. "Actually, Tori told me. She saw Lucas just as he was leaving."

Miranda felt guilty that she'd forgotten to call her friend, in all the excitement of seeing Shannon.

"Tori had to go home and try to get some rest before her shift at the Silver Spur. She said to tell you she'd be in touch, or you can come by the Spur later if you feel up to it."

Miranda wanted to believe Tori planned to go in to work, rather than asking for the night off, out of loyalty to her boss. But she had a feeling it had more to do with Tori not being ready to face Miranda in private yet.

"You need to get some rest, too," Shannon said. "Lord knows, I plan to sleep for the next two days."

"I think I've gotten a second wind," she answered. "Or maybe it's more like a third or a fourth."

Her sister sat up. "I'm so sorry I put you both through all this," she said. "Especially what Mom told me about you two seeing that note and the photos. I thought I'd be home before Tori gave them to you, and I hated even leaving them with her. I just felt like I didn't have a choice."

"I'm not even sure what happened," Paige said. "Fill me in on what you told the police."

Shannon told them her story. When she got to the part about hiding at the cabin, Miranda interrupted.

"What in the world happened there today, by the way? I about died when I burst in and saw all that broken glass and everything."

"Clint was at the Truck Inn when Fae and Mae heard the call come in through dispatch for the state police," Shannon said. "I guess he heard the cabin mentioned, and he put it together. He broke in through the window…scared me half to death." Her voice trembled. "It took me a minute to realize he'd been the one sending me the threats. The note, the photos. I threw everything I could reach at him. But before I could make it to the front door, he forced me out the back."

"But why?" Paige asked. "What does he have against us?"

"I was testifying against his former jail buddy," Shannon said. "He got awful loose lipped…. That's what scared me most. I knew he wouldn't be telling me everything unless he planned to see me dead."

She shuddered.

"When Lonnie was arrested for the rape and murder of Jo Ella Jamison, he contacted Clint and offered him a lot of money to make sure I didn't testify."

"Dear heaven," Paige said. "I would never have believed Clint capable of this…. Taking money… It's so premeditated."

"I know," Shannon murmured.

"What did Clint plan to do?" Miranda asked. She was afraid she already knew the answer.

"Well, at first he only tried to scare me into hiding, and it worked. But then, when he realized everyone was looking for me, he decided it might be best to get rid of me, like Lonnie had wanted him to do in the first place."

"Was it just Clint?" Miranda asked. "Or were others involved?"

"Just him," Shannon said. "Lonnie had something on him... You're never going to believe this." She hesitated. "Clint bragged that the two of them had been involved in a meth lab a couple of years ago. Now, please, don't tell Lucas this or he'll never be able to get past it.... Clint shot a cop.... He escaped, but Lonnie was arrested. And—and the cop died. That's what Lonnie had on Clint." Shannon reached out and gripped her mother's hand. "He joined the search party to make sure he got to me first... So he could get rid of me."

"He was actually going to kill you." Miranda slowly shook her head. Lucas's brother! That he could really do such a thing...

Shannon lowered her gaze, her face pale. "If you and Lucas hadn't come along, Miranda—"

"Don't think about that," Paige said hastily.

"But why did he leave you tied up?" Miranda asked. "I don't understand."

"He'd gagged me and tied my hands when he walked me up there—"

"But why didn't he just...just shoot you in the cabin," Miranda forced herself to ask.

"He was hoping no one would ever find my...my body," Shannon explained.

"Then once we got there, he tied my feet, and he was about to—to shoot me when he heard you all coming up the trail. You know the rest."

Miranda shivered. Clint could've just as easily shot her sister. Why he'd chosen not to, or why he hadn't gone ahead and shot Lucas, she didn't know. Maybe he'd had last-minute second thoughts.

"Well, I'm just glad it's all over," Paige said. She leaned forward and hugged Shannon. "Don't you ever do something like that again, young lady."

"I already told her," Miranda said.

"No worries there, Mom. Believe me. But it's not over." Shannon chewed her bottom lip. "I still have to testify against Lonnie Masterson."

"Yes, but it's going to be all right now," Miranda stated, joining her mother on the couch. "Clint's locked up, and if Lonnie has any more crazy ideas about sending his buddies after you, he'll have to go through me to do it."

Shannon laughed softly. "Thanks, Mia." Then she frowned. "You'll have to testify against Clint."

"With pleasure," Miranda said.

"I wonder how Lucas is handling all of this," Paige murmured. "I didn't get to talk to him before he left the hospital."

Miranda thought of the way he'd practically run her out of the emergency room. "I think it bothers him more than he wants to admit," she said. "It can't be easy, having family like that."

"That's for sure," her mom declared. "Maybe you were better off not to marry into that bunch, after all."

Miranda's heart ached. Was she? Lucas wasn't anything like the rest of the Blaylocks.

She stood. "I'm going to make some coffee. You drink your juice and rest, Shannon."

"Yes, Mother." Shannon rolled her eyes.

Miranda told herself she was lucky to be rid of Lucas and all the pain he'd caused her.

But she longed to be with him, to never let him go.

LUCAS SAT IN THE DARK in his living room, nursing a beer. He hardly ever touched alcohol, but today he needed it. He'd gone to work after leaving the hospital, and had pulled his entire shift—in spite of reprimands from his dispatcher and his deputies—before finally going home.

One cat lay at his feet, two more curled up on the couch with him. The white kitten he called Jack Frost eased its way onto his lap, making mud pies with its paws against his leg. The little thing purred as loudly as a tiger. Lucas scratched Frost's ears.

Garrett had gotten a full confession out of Clint. He'd taken it down while Lucas watched and listened, Frank a formal witness just to be sure no one accused them of impartiality. They'd gotten it in writing and on videotape. Once Clint had been escorted to lockup, waiting for the bus that would take him to the county jail, Lucas had played that tape over and over.

Clint admitted he hadn't done it just for the money Lonnie Masterson promised to pay him. He'd done it to hurt Lucas. Clint had taken extra pleasure in going after Shannon once Lucas had arrested him for abusing Dena. That admission gave Lucas pause. Apparently his estranged brother realized how deeply connected he felt to the Ward family…even when Lucas hadn't known it.

He slowly shook his head. He couldn't understand why or how his brother could hate him this much. Of course, domestic violence charges was the least of Clint's worries right now. He faced charges of kidnapping, burglary and assaulting a police officer with a deadly weapon, among others. Lucas could take satisfaction in knowing that his brother was locked up where he couldn't hurt Dena anymore, but now he wondered how she'd make it without the salary Clint earned working down at the sawmill.

Lucas vowed to make sure she didn't want for anything, but still, where did all this leave her? Married to a man in prison. Would she stay with him…wait for him to do his time and get out, only to abuse her again? Lucas hated to think of the day Clint would walk the streets again, even if it was twenty years from now.

Miranda. She'd made him madder than a wasp in a shaken nest more than once. Yet he had to admire her devotion to her sister. A devotion that had led her to risk her own life, making sure Shannon was safe.

What would it be like to have family like that? He'd never know.

LUCAS WOKE UP TO THE sound of knocking. For a moment, he was disoriented. Had he fallen asleep and missed going out with the search party? Then he remembered. Shannon Ward was home.

Rubbing a hand over his face, he made his way to the door and opened it. Dena stood on the other side.

"Morning," she said. "Can I come in?"

"Sure, but I've only got a minute. I'm running late for work."

Dena's gaze roamed the still-darkened room as she stepped through the doorway. "Wow. This is some place."

Lucas grunted and pulled the curtains open. Suddenly, he realized his own sister-in-law had never been inside his house.

"Guess you had a hard day yesterday, huh?" she asked.

"I'm sure it was no picnic for you, either. I'm sorry things had to turn out this way, Dena."

"Don't apologize, Lucas. Clint is a real loser, and I should've woken up to that a long time ago." She hesitated. "I wanted to let you know that I'm planning to divorce him and move out of state. If I stay here, I know I'll break down and go to the prison and visit Clint. I'll lose my nerve, and I don't want to do that."

"Glad to hear it."

"Do you think they're going to let him out on bail?" Fear pinched her otherwise pretty features.

"I doubt it. He's a pretty good flight risk, given his fear of Lonnie Masterson. Plus his previous record of DUI, domestic violence... I don't think the judge will let him out."

Dena breathed an audible sigh of relief.

"Where will you go?"

She shrugged. "I haven't thought quite that far ahead. But I've got cousins in Colorado and California. Probably one of the two." Dena had become estranged from her parents years ago when she married Clint. They hated him, and wouldn't have anything to do with giving their blessing to their daughter's marriage.

Lucas couldn't blame them.

"I also wanted to give you this," Dena said. "I don't know if it's important, but I thought you ought to have it."

Lucas held out his hand as she passed him a small object. He looked down at his palm and saw that it was an unusual button, probably off a ladies' blouse. He looked up at Dena quizzically. "Where'd this come from, and why should I have it?"

"My cat was playing with it on the steps."

The big gray cat, playing with what Lucas had thought was a pebble. Had it been the button?

"It's off a blouse I made for Shannon," Dena said.

"For her birthday one year, back when we were just out of high school." She smiled sadly. "Back when we were still hanging around together. Clint gradually made sure he ran off all of my friends, Shannon in particular, since she was Miranda's sister, and you two…well, you know."

"I don't understand," Lucas said, frowning. "What would your cat be doing with a button off Shannon's old blouse?"

"It was always her favorite," Dena said. "I made it to last. Not like the cheap junk you buy in the stores today." She thrust her hands into the back pockets of her jeans. "I went to the jail yesterday, and I asked Clint point-blank where that button came from, and what it was doing on our porch. At first he tried to lie to me, but then I think he realized that he's going to be in prison for a long time, without a friend in the world."

She looked down at her feet. "He doesn't know I'm leaving. Anyway, he told me he'd been watching Shannon for a long time. And that he'd planned to do something to her for Lonnie weeks ago. He…he took her blouse out of her bedroom one night when she left her window open. Can you believe that? That he'd have the nerve to go into Miss Paige's house like that, when they were all sleeping?"

A chill raced down Lucas's spine, causing the hairs on his neck to stand on end. He closed his hand into a fist, wishing he could have a few minutes alone in a room with Clint…same as Jack McQuaid had wished for the other night when Lucas had talked to him at the Silver Spur. But that wasn't right. Justice was what Lucas stood for, and he'd gotten that.

So why did he feel so empty?

"I'm still scared some idiot judge will let him out on bail," Dena said.

"Don't be afraid. I'm here to protect you, Dena. And if you need any money, just let me know."

"Thanks, Lucas, but I'm fine. I've got a little tucked away that Clint doesn't know about. Plus I'm selling his truck, for what it's worth."

Lucas laughed. "That piece of junk? You'll be lucky to get scrap metal dollar out of it."

"Fine by me. It might be sort of fun to watch that crusher come down on it."

He grinned.

"Well, I'd better let you get off to work," Dena said. She stood on tiptoe and planted a kiss on his cheek. "Thanks for everything, Lucas. I'll keep in touch."

"Do that." Lucas stood in the doorway, watching her leave. She gave a little finger wave as she drove away.

Lucas closed the door and headed for the shower.

The button burned a hole in the palm of his hand. It made him even happier that Clint was behind bars.

CHAPTER SEVENTEEN

MIRANDA SPENT THE NEXT two days after Shannon had come home, at the Rocking W. She was afraid to leave her sister, even though she knew that fear was irrational. Clint was behind bars, as was Lonnie Masterson—and with phone privileges suspended until after his trial. And it wasn't as though her mom and sister were helpless.

Still, she couldn't get thoughts of the unidentified woman over in Cameron County out of her mind. Somebody was responsible for her death, and from what Miranda had gathered, listening to the local news with her mom and sister last night, Clint was not believed to be that person. What he'd done to Shannon had personal motivation.

So who had killed that poor girl? Miranda had to admit that Lucas's concern had rubbed off on her. She'd never given much thought before to Tori working late at the Silver Spur. But now she found herself worrying about her friend, in spite of Tori's reassurances. They'd patched up the hurt feelings between them, and everything felt normal again. Except Miranda's worries.

She drove to the Spur that Saturday night, before it got dark outside. The band didn't start playing until eight o'clock. Miranda sat at the bar and ordered a beer. She could use one.

"So," Tori said, pushing a frosted mug of draft in front of her, "you gonna hang out here every time I'm working?"

"Until whoever killed that girl is caught."

"Miranda…babe." Tori laid her hand over Miranda's, looking her straight in the eye. "You need to worry about yourself. You live out on that big ole ranch alone. You think I don't worry about you?"

"I've got my dogs, and a gun or two."

"And I've got a shotgun, plus Fae and Mae." Tori grinned, and added sotto voce, "And a derringer in my purse. So quit being such a momma hen."

Miranda sighed, and was about to argue the point further, when she caught sight of Lucas coming in. She stiffened.

"Hi," he said, sliding onto the bar stool beside her. He wore his uniform. "Give me a Coke, would you please, Tori?"

"Coming right up."

"I'm sorry I was short with you the other day," he said to Miranda.

"Were you? I didn't notice."

"Glad to hear it," he said dryly. "So how's Shannon doing?"

"Pretty good, all things considered." How could

she stay mad at him? "I really am grateful for everything, Lucas."

"Did you ever consider becoming an officer?"

"No, thanks. I think I've had enough excitement to last me a lifetime."

Lucas sipped the Coke Tori set in front of him, waiting until she moved down the bar before speaking. "Miranda, I stopped by here to ask you something."

"Yeah? What's that?"

"Would you go with me to the animal shelter on Monday?"

It was the last thing she'd expected him to say. "The animal shelter? Well, sure. Are you adopting another cat?"

He shook his head. "Actually, it occurred to me that your mom and Shannon ought to have some dogs on the ranch. You know, watchdogs, like your Aussies. I'd like to get them a couple, as a sort of welcome-home gift for Shannon, and for your mom…just because." His face reddened. "Hope I'm not overstepping my bounds, but…" He hesitated, as though debating something. "Miranda, my brother was stalking Shannon long before he kidnapped her."

Miranda nearly choked on her beer. "Stalking her?"

Lucas nodded, then went on to explain Dena's visit.

Miranda felt sick, and glad she was already sitting down. "Please tell me you're not serious."

"As a heart attack. I can't be your sister's and your

mother's constant shadow, or yours, either. It makes me feel better knowing you've got those dogs."

"And my gun," Miranda said. "Mom's got a shot-gun, two rifles and two handguns."

"Maybe so, but she still didn't hear Clint when he came into Shannon's room."

"When did he do that?" Miranda's hand shook, and she took another sip of her beer.

"I don't know, exactly. So, will you go with me to pick out the dogs?"

"Yeah, I will," she said. "Mom used to have a dog—a husky—but he was old, and she lost him last summer. I guess she just wasn't ready to replace him."

"Well," Lucas said, "let's hope she's ready now."

LUCAS CAME TO MIRANDA'S place on Monday morning, right after she'd finished her chores. She rode with him to the shelter. It made her sad to see how many wonderful dogs were there. A border collie mix caught her eye. But she was so sweet, Miranda couldn't see her in the role of watchdog.

She and Lucas finally decided on a pair of Aus-tralian shepherd German shepherd mixes, six-month old littermates. Lucas filled out the paperwork, while Miranda walked back and looked at the border collie one more time. She was two years old, mostly white with black patches over her body. She had one comical marking over her left eye—a black patch that made her look as if she were wearing eye shadow. She woofed at Miranda.

"All right," Miranda said. "I guess Tuck and Smudge could use some more company."

Miranda helped Lucas secure the Aussies in the back of his truck in some airline crates she'd bought. The crates would come in handy for her mom in housebreaking the pups. But the border collie rode in the front seat between them.

Lucas patted the dog's head. "I'm sure your killer hounds are going to be thrilled."

"They'll get used to her," Miranda said. She laughed. "Look at that tail. It never stops wagging. I think I'll call her Happy."

"I think I'll let you take the dogs out to Paige," Lucas said. "I don't think she likes me very much. She might receive the pups better if she thinks they're coming from you."

Miranda started to protest, but then remembered her mom's remark the other day. *Maybe you were better off not marrying into that bunch, after all, Miranda.* "All right. If you're sure."

He nodded. Just then, his cell phone rang. Lucas answered, listening for a few minutes. He spoke quietly, then hung up, his expression serious.

"What is it?" Miranda's pulse raced. She hoped nothing else was wrong.

"That was Sheriff Runyon, over in Silver Creek. They identified their Jane Doe—a twenty-one-year-old Jana Wilson. She lived about fifty miles from Silver Creek—with her parents. They'd gone on a vacation without her, and just got home."

"That's awful." Miranda clamped a hand to her mouth, unable to imagine how the poor couple must feel. "They still don't know who killed her?"

Lucas shook his head. "Not yet."

Minutes later, they pulled into Miranda's driveway. Smudge and Tuck chased the truck, excited to see the dogs they'd already scented. Lucas helped Miranda transfer the big pups to her truck, and stayed for a few minutes while she introduced Happy to the Aussies. Tuck wagged his tail, but Smudge stiffened to a dominating posture and hooked a front paw over Happy's middle. "Hey," Miranda scolded. "Be nice."

"Where are you going to put her?" Lucas asked. "I mean, you can't just turn her loose, right?"

"I've got a dog run out beside the barn. I have to put Tuck and Smudge in there once in a while. Happy can stay there for a few days until she adjusts." Miranda led the dog around to the far side of the barn and into the chain-link run, and gave her food and water.

Happy stood on the doghouse and barked at Tuck and Smudge, her tail going a mile a minute.

"Looks like she fits her name," Lucas said. He shifted uncomfortably, and for a moment, Miranda thought he was going to say something else to her. But then he shoved his hands into his pockets. "Guess I'd better be going. I need to run by the station and make sure Garrett and the others heard about Jana Wilson."

Miranda nodded. "Okay. Lucas, thanks for getting the dogs. Are you sure I can't pay you for them?"

"Nope. My gift." He touched the brim of his hat. "See you later."

Miranda watched him walk away, still wondering exactly where she stood with Lucas.

She drove the pups out to the Rocking W. Paige was in the arena with Shannon, watching her work a new horse. Her mother's face glowed, and Shannon looked so happy on the mare's back that no one would've guessed she'd recently suffered a traumatic experience.

Except for the dark circles under her eyes.

"Hey, Mom," Miranda said. "Nice mare."

"Isn't she?" Paige kept her eyes on the blue roan. "Chet found her at an auction Saturday. He got her for a steal."

"Well, I'm glad you're in the mood for new animals, because I brought you something."

"What—did you find a good horse, too?"

Miranda shook her head, motioning for Paige to follow her. She led her to the truck.

Paige peered into the dog kennels. "What have you got here?"

"They're sisters," Miranda said. "Do you want them?" She held her breath. What if her mom wasn't ready for another dog yet?

What in the world would Miranda do with five dogs?

But Paige's face lit up. "Where did you get them? They're adorable." She poked her fingers through the doors of the crates. "Hi, babies. How are you? Huh?"

The black-and-tan sister wagged her tail, and the one that had merle markings licked Paige's finger.

"I got them from the animal shelter," Miranda said. "Actually, Lucas bought them for you."

Paige straightened. "Lucas? For me?" She couldn't have looked more surprised if Miranda had told her the dogs were a gift from Elvis. "Why would he do that?"

Miranda told her about Clint. "But you can't tell Shannon," she said quietly. "I don't want to put her through any more than what she's already been through."

Paige clenched her fists. "I swear, if they don't put that son of a bitch in prison for life, I'm going to kill him myself." She took a deep breath. "I agree with you. Let's not tell Shannon. But I still can't believe...Lucas." She shook her head. "The man never ceases to amaze me. Maybe I've misjudged him." She smiled at Miranda. "People change."

"Yeah, they do."

Miranda only wished she could make Lucas believe it.

CHAPTER EIGHTEEN

"I'M AS NERVOUS AS a long-tailed cat in a room full of rocking chairs," Shannon said as she stood outside the courtroom with Miranda, Paige and Tori.

"You'll do just fine," her sister said. "And that scum-sucking creep Masterson will be put away, hopefully for life."

Just days ago, the news channels had been flooded with the story of Jana Wilson's murder and the arrest of a man in the next county charged with the crime. A copycat killer, as Miranda had originally suspected. A guy who frequented local bars and who appeared on the evening news wearing a ball cap and blue jeans.

Miranda shivered, recalling Jack McQuaid's description of the man who'd started to follow Shannon outside the Silver Spur the night she'd witnessed Jo Ella's abduction.

The past twelve days had sped by, and Miranda hadn't seen or talked to Lucas since he'd taken her to the animal shelter. Had he withdrawn from her again? She saw him now as he entered the courthouse, not here to testify but, like her, to observe.

Miranda couldn't bring herself to go over and talk to him. She was starting to like having him in her life way too much.

She'd been at the courthouse the past two days, listening to testimony from various witnesses during the trial of the man who'd been responsible for her sister's near brush with death. The man who'd hired Clint to stalk her. Miranda planned to be here every day, looking him straight in the eye, until it was over. As a witness, Shannon, however, couldn't watch the trial. All witnesses were sequestered from hearing one another's testimony. But today, Shannon would be called to the stand. She was the final witness on the prosecution's list.

The bailiff opened the doors to let in the spectators. Miranda paused to give her sister one last hug.

"Good luck," she murmured, "not that you'll need it. You're going to do fine."

"I hope so," Shannon said. She set her jaw and went on in.

Miranda entered the courtroom with her mother and Tori right behind her. Fae and Mae were already inside, and had front row seats saved. They sat glaring at the back of Masterson's head, and as though he was able to sense their stares, he turned around, meeting twin looks of pure hatred. Nobody messed with the Lambert sisters, or any of their kin or friends. Especially if it meant involving Tori—who they'd quickly forgiven for deceiving them.

Miranda would love to take a swing or two at Lonnie herself—at the very least.

Her palms grew damp when it came Shannon's turn to take the stand. But her sister held up like a trooper, looking Lonnie straight in the eye when she identified him and told the jury what she'd witnessed the night Jo Ella was abducted and murdered. When her testimony was done, Shannon rejoined Miranda and Tori, and the three slipped quietly outside. Fae, Mae and Paige followed.

"Oh my God," Shannon said, sinking onto a bench near the door. "I'm so glad that's over."

Tori lit up a cigarette. "Me, too. I felt like I was up on that stand with you."

"Put that thing out!" Fae demanded, waving at the cloud of cigarette smoke. "It'll give you lung cancer."

Tori sucked on the cigarette, moaning with pleasure. "But I'll die a contented woman."

"Not hardly," Mae scolded. "Don't you remember what happened to your aunt Tootie? Smoked two packs a day all her life…."

Miranda let their words fade to the back of her mind as Lucas came out of the courthouse. He merely nodded at them as he passed. Miranda's pulse raced. She was angry at his indifference. Disappointed he hadn't stopped.

She watched him get in the Blazer and drive away.

"Wonder where he's off to?" Paige murmured. She leaned over and whispered in Miranda's ear,

"Honey, I know you're dying to talk to him. Go on." She grinned. "You can catch him."

Miranda managed a smile. She did need to air the thoughts keeping her awake, one way or another.

In her truck, Miranda let her mind wander as she drove after Lucas. Did he have any feelings at all for her? He'd sure made her think so, the way he'd made love to her. But then, she'd been the one to initiate that. What man in his right mind would say no to a willing woman?

It took her a few minutes to realize where Lucas was going, as he finally headed up Cemetery Road and pulled into the tiny Sage Bend Gardens. He got out and glanced Miranda's way before walking over to his mother's grave.

Miranda parked beside his Blazer. Lucas's father hadn't killed Laura Blaylock with his own hands, but he might as well have. She'd died from a stress-related heart condition at the age of forty-five, exacerbated by Clyde Blaylock's abuse.

Miranda opened her door and got out. She would never forget the funeral. Lucas had lost his temper and punched his father. It was the only time she'd ever seen Lucas commit an act of violence.

It wasn't long after that when Clyde had gone to prison. Lucas had been nineteen, Clint seventeen.

No wonder Lucas hadn't been ready to marry when he was twenty-three. What had Miranda been thinking? She walked up beside him and stood without speaking. For a moment, she didn't think he was going to acknowledge her presence.

"She should've left him," Lucas said. "Should've taken us when we were kids and left. Maybe then she'd still be here. And maybe my brother would've turned out differently."

"Maybe so," Miranda said. "It's sad she had to die so young."

"At least Dena's wised up." Finally, he looked at Miranda. "She's leaving Clint. Moving out of state."

"You're kidding."

"Nope. She's leaving this weekend."

"I'm glad to hear that," Miranda said.

For a moment, they were silent. "You're not like him, you know. You're not anything like your father."

"That's not true. I've got a bad temper. I wanted to knock the tar out of Clint that night I put him in jail, when I saw him hit Dena." He gave a dry laugh. "I came pretty close. I've wanted to punch him out on more than one occasion."

"But that's the difference," Miranda said. "You might have wanted to, but you didn't. You might even have a bad temper, but you've learned to control it."

"Maybe."

"Damn it, Lucas!" Miranda wanted to shake him. "You're making me so mad, I'm about to lose *my* temper." She spread her arms wide. "See, I've got one, too. Doesn't mean I'm going to haul off and smack you. Why can't you see you're a man of integrity? You're the kind of man any woman would be lucky to have. And if you'd stop being so stubborn for just a minute, and take a good hard look at yourself, maybe you'd see that, too."

He only stared at her.

"I give up." At a loss, Miranda turned and stormed away.

Lucas would never see things the way she did, never realize that she loved him more than anything in the world.

And he would never come to believe he was the good, kind and loving man Miranda saw when she looked into his eyes.

The man she wanted to spend the rest of her life with.

MIRANDA SPENT THE WEEKEND with Tori at the Silver Spur—on Friday, which was Tori's night off, and again on Saturday, when she had to work the bar. Both times Miranda drank Coke all night and danced with every cowboy who asked her. Some were good-looking, some not. None were Lucas.

"I think you need something stronger than that to wash him out of your head," Tori said, setting another Coke in front of her after Miranda came off the dance floor, where she'd done a lively two-step with Jack McQuaid.

"I doubt all the whiskey in Tennessee could," Miranda declared. "Is this what a rebroken heart feels like?"

"I wouldn't know," Tori said. "I've never been one to settle for one man." She gave Miranda a wink. "Why buy the bull when you can ride the rodeo circuit for free?"

"Tori!"

Her friend laughed. "You've got to move on, girl!"

"Maybe you're right." Miranda sighed. "Hey, want to see a movie this week? The new Brad Pitt film is playing over at the mall in Pine Bluff."

"Sounds good. I'm celebrating all week, you know." Tori leaned forward and spoke directly into Miranda's ear to be heard over the music. "Lucas thinks I'll just get probation and community service for lying to the police. He decided not to write me up for…well, you know." She looked around to be sure no one was listening. "He said, and I quote, 'After all, Tori, your heart was in the right place, if not your six-shooter.'"

Miranda laughed. "That sounds like Lucas." Then she sobered. "If your aunts found out that part…"

"Oh, brother." Tori clamped a hand to her breast. "They'd skin me alive." She glanced over at a couple of cowboys who'd bellied up to the bar, and waved. "Be right back." She hurried off to wait on them.

Thinking of Lucas, Miranda suddenly didn't feel so much like partying. She waited until Tori came back, then pushed her half-finished Coke glass her friend's way. "I think I'm going to call it a night."

"This early?" Tori frowned. "Man, first you turn into a teetotaler on me, and then you go home to bed at—" she peered at her watch "—ten-fifteen? Sheesh, Miranda. You must be getting old."

She chuckled. "Maybe so." Too old to be pining away for the same man for over a decade. She handed Tori a five. "I'll see you later."

Outside, Miranda fired up her truck and put on some loud country music. Something sad about broken hearts. She sang along as she headed home, feeling more and more melancholy as she drove. But when she got to her house, she did a double take.

Lucas's Blazer was in her driveway. Miranda parked beside it and got out. Where were Tuck and Smudge? Better yet, where was Lucas? And suddenly she knew.

Trying not to look as desperate as she felt, Miranda made her way out behind the barn, through the gate to the creek. Sure enough, Lucas sat by the water.

And next to him sat Tuck and Smudge.

"What have you done to my watchdogs?" Miranda demanded, dropping onto the creek bank on the other side of Tuck.

Lucas gave her a crooked grin that melted her heart. "I fed them hot dogs."

"Hot dogs?" Miranda rolled her eyes. "You've got

to be kidding." She ruffled her dogs' fur. "Some watchdogs you are—caving in to bribery."

"I don't know why I didn't think of it before," Lucas said. "Oh, and I gave some to Happy, too. It made her quit barking."

"Does this mean you plan to continue the habit of trespassing on my property? Now that you've got my dogs in your hip pocket? Or should I say, in a hot dog packet?"

He laughed. "Maybe… I guess I've been pretty hard-headed about this whole thing between me and you."

Miranda held her breath.

"It's just that I'm not sure I'm the marrying kind."

She gave an unladylike snort. "I guess I figured that one out a long time ago."

"Miranda, I only did what I thought was best for you."

"Well, you hurt me, Lucas. Right here." She placed a fist against her chest.

"I'm mighty ashamed of that." He edged closer, nudging Tuck out of the way. Reaching out, he gently touched her cheek. "I love you, Miranda. And I'll never again make you a promise I can't keep. Do you trust me enough to believe me?"

"Lucas…"

He placed his fingers beneath her chin and slowly raised it, covering her mouth with his. He brushed featherlight kisses across her lips, and Miranda closed her eyes and kissed him back, savoring the familiar taste and feel of him, wishing things could be as ideal forever as they felt right now. Knowing that wasn't likely to happen.

"I love you, Miranda," he whispered again. "Say you love me, too."

She groaned, grasping his wrist to hold him still. "I do love you, Lucas. I always have. But there's more to it than that."

"Please, Miranda. I'm begging you to give me another chance. Let me love you, sweetheart. Just let me love you." He took her into his arms, and Miranda relaxed against him.

With a sigh, she draped her wrists around his neck, pulling him close, loving the way his warm, hard body felt against hers. Gradually, he eased her onto her back in the long, soft grass. Miranda felt the years slip away....

"Lucas," she said, kissing him over and over. "I want things to be the way they used to be."

"Uh-uh," he said, smiling when she drew back. "Things are going to be even better." He brushed the hair away from her temple. "We were kids back then. We're all grown-up now, and I think I finally understand what I've been running from."

"Yeah?" She held her breath, half-afraid of what he might say.

"I was so busy being scared I might turn out to be like Clint and Dad that I forgot who I was."

"And now?"

"You bring out all the best in me, Miranda. I've spent the past few days feeling so empty inside. Like something was missing. That something was you." He kissed her again.

"Then let me fill you up," she whispered. Miranda closed her eyes and they kissed.

At some point, she heard Smudge and Tuck lope away through the grass, in pursuit of more interesting activities. No wonder Lucas had won them over. He was an easy man to get close to, once you gave him half a chance. She wanted to give him more than half a chance.

He undressed her, there beneath the stars, with the cottonwoods overhead. Just as he once had. But this time, his hands were not those of an inexperienced boy. They were the hands of a grown man, sure of what he wanted. And he wanted her.

Miranda unsnapped Lucas's shirt and slid it off, taking time to run her palms along the muscles of his shoulders and biceps. He looked so fine in the moonlight, cowboy hat, shirtless, tight blue jeans.

Lucas tossed his shirt aside, followed by the rest of his clothes. He bunched his shirt up and used it for a pillow to place beneath her head. Miranda's heart swelled. "Now that's something I don't remember from the last time we were here."

He laughed softly. "I know how to treat a lady."

"Do you, now?" She reached for him. "Why don't you show me."

"Gladly."

He stretched across her, still holding and kissing her. Miranda lay back and enjoyed his ministrations. Last time, she'd wanted to dominate him, punish him. This time, she wanted to lie in his arms and let him do whatever he wanted to her.

And when he entered her, Miranda moaned and wrapped her tongue around his. With her legs around him, she pulled him closer, moving in slow gyrations against him. Creating a friction that drove them both crazy.

They climaxed as one. Afterward, Miranda lay with her head tucked against Lucas's shoulder, his arm around her, hers draped across his chest. She ran her hand over the light dusting of hair, enjoying the feel of his hot, damp skin beneath her palm. "That was…"

"Phenomenal," he finished.

She laughed. "Yes. I'd say so."

He chuckled softly, pulling her closer still. "I love you, woman."

"And I love you, Sheriff. I knew it would be fun to get you naked again."

"You don't say. And how often did you think about doing that?"

"Oh, just about every time I saw you."

"Really? Well, I guess that makes us even."

Now it was her turn to chuckle. The two of them lay quietly, staring up at the stars. Miranda closed her eyes and let the feeling of relaxation seep through every inch of her body.

And then it occurred to her. Lucas hadn't asked her to marry him. Hadn't made any sort of commitment. He'd only told her he'd keep his promises from now on.

What were those promises to be?

Miranda drifted off to sleep, still wondering.

LUCAS DOZED WITH MIRANDA in his arms. Never in his life had he felt so fulfilled, so content. Loving her was the best thing that had ever happened to him. He was only sorry it had taken him so long to realize it. So, what now? Did he dare ask her—for the second time—to marry him? Deciding it might be better to wait, Lucas snuggled against her, nuzzling her neck. He became aroused in an instant, and kissed her awake. She moaned and rolled into him, gladly welcoming his body again.

They made love, slowly and leisurely. There was something to be said about no longer being twenty. He knew how to take his time with her, knew how to draw out the moment and make it great for both of them.

When they were finished, Lucas took pleasure in the contented sigh that came from Miranda. "Are you as happy as you sound?" he asked.

"At least. You?"

"Without a doubt." He wrapped his arms around her and kissed her. "But I suppose we should get up and get dressed. After all, you never know when someone might radio in for backup."

"And it wouldn't do for the sheriff of Sage Bend to be caught with his pants down…literally." She laughed.

They dressed, and he held her for a few minutes, standing on the creek bank, before he finally turned to leave. "I love you, Miranda," he repeated. "I'll call you tomorrow."

"You'd better."

He practically floated as he walked through her back gate toward his Blazer.

And then Tuck and Smudge dived in and heeled him.

"Hey!" He frowned, dodging their quick, sharp nips. "I thought we were friends."

From the other side of the gate, Miranda laughed. "Some things never change," she called. "Good night, Lucas."

CHAPTER NINETEEN

MIRANDA WOKE UP early Monday morning to a threatening, cloudy sky. Hurriedly, she dressed and took care of her animals, grabbing an apple as she went out the door. She needed to go to town and get some feed, and if she didn't hustle, the rain would beat her to the draw. She couldn't haul grain and dog food in a wet pickup bed.

But before Miranda could get there, the skies opened up and rain poured down in what looked like a gully washer. Oh, well. She'd just have to settle for buying whatever amount of dog food and grain she could shove into the front seat. It would be enough to tide her over.

As she rounded a corner downtown, a building caught her eye: the white-frame church where she and Lucas had meant to hold their wedding. Why had she come this way? On a whim, Miranda parked her truck in front of it and walked up to the front door.

Pastor Hill never locked the church. He lived in the modest, white frame house next door, and kept a watchful eye on things. He proclaimed to leave God's house open for all who might need to come in.

Thank goodness there weren't any homeless in Sage Bend. Miranda smiled at the thought of Pastor Hill waking up to find a dozen people sleeping on his pews. Knowing his kind heart, he'd take them all in, like the stray dogs he fed.

Miranda felt ashamed she hadn't gone to Sunday service in more time than she could count. She'd stopped attending once she'd been humiliated here, and somehow never found a way back to any church.

As she walked down the ruby-colored carpet between the rows of worn pews, she felt right at home. Above her, a skylight of stained glass made the cloud-darkened day seem a little brighter. A brass cross hung on the far wall above the pulpit, and three sets of windows on either side lined the walls, letting in what little light there was. Outside, Miranda heard the rumble of thunder. She went to the small offerings box at the rear of the church and stuffed a handful of bills into it. Then she sat in the back.

"Sorry, God," she said out loud. "I haven't meant to stay away so long." She knelt in the pew, and gave a prayer of thanks for Shannon's safe return. Then she simply sat and absorbed the silence.

In her memory, she could see the flowers decorating every aisle; see Lucas's best friends, Jake and Corky, standing at the front with Pastor Hill. It had been a small ceremony. At least, they'd intended for it to be small.

Miranda got up from the pew and walked to the

aisle, looking straight ahead. She remembered the puzzlement she'd felt when she'd entered the church and realized that Lucas wasn't there. Somehow, the eighty-five-year-old woman who'd played the organ hadn't realized it, and she'd struck up "Here Comes the Bride."

Confused, Miranda had started her walk down the aisle. But only her friends and the pastor had stood there, waiting to meet her. *Where was Lucas?*

Miranda closed her eyes, breathing in the clean, somehow holy scent of the church. The smells of worn, well-used hymn books and lemon furniture polish drifted over her.

"I wanted to kick his butt back then," Tori said from behind her, "and I'll do it today if that man has done something to hurt you again."

Miranda opened her eyes and turned. Her friend stood there with an armload of buckets, rags and cleaning products.

"Tori, what are you doing here?" Miranda nodded at the mop and buckets. "You're cleaning?"

"Yep. Thought I'd get a jump on my community service." She rolled her eyes. "Lily Tate normally does it, but she's out sick, so I promised Pastor Hill I'd take over for her this week. Aunt Fae and Aunt Mae rearranged my schedule so it would work out." She dropped her load where the carpet met hardwood flooring. "The bathrooms in the basement are the toughest, especially the men's room." She wrinkled her nose. "You'd think good Christians would know how to aim, but I guess they're all just cowboys underneath."

Miranda couldn't help but chuckle.

Tori sat on the edge of a pew. "Now tell me what you're doing in here. Tormenting yourself?"

Miranda shrugged. "I don't know. I guess it's because Lucas and I are back together—at least I'm pretty sure we are."

Tori raised her brows. "Pretty sure? Either you are or you aren't."

"Okay, we are. Only I'm not certain what his intentions are, and I was stupid not to ask." She smacked her hand against her thigh. "I just leaped before I looked, and now I don't know what to do."

"You slept with him," Tori said accusingly. "Miranda, how could you?" Then she quirked her mouth. "Actually, how could you not? He's mighty yummy." Then she clamped one hand to her mouth and looked apologetically up at the cross. "Sorry."

Miranda laughed. "Yeah, he's yummy all right." She looked around. "I feel sort of weird talking about this here."

"What was I thinking?" Tori glanced at her watch. "Meet me at the diner at eleven and we'll have an early lunch. You can tell me all about it then."

"Okay," Miranda said. "But only if we take our orders to go. I'm not about to let Fae and Mae overhear."

"Takeout it is."

But once she was out at her truck, Miranda wasn't sure she wanted to talk about what had happened between her and Lucas at all. She must be out of her mind to risk another broken heart. But it was too late to do anything about it.

She drove to the feed store and bought a hundred pounds of grain and fifty pounds of dog food. The rain had let up, but the truck bed was soaked, so she loaded them into the cab and took off. As she drove past the sheriff's office, she saw Lucas's Blazer and pulled into the parking lot on impulse. Taking a deep breath, Miranda went inside.

He sat behind his desk, frowning at some paperwork. But when he saw her, his eyes lit up, and Miranda realized how much she loved him.

"Hey," he said. "What are you doing out on a soggy morning like this?"

"I needed feed," she said, shutting his office door behind her. She sat in the chair on the other side of his desk. "And I needed to talk to you. I didn't realize it until I drove past the church."

Lucas immediately became serious. "The church?"

"Yep. I hadn't been in it since…well, since our wedding that never happened. Lucas, I've got to know, are we back together? Are we dating? Or are we just having sex? I'm so confused."

"Miranda, I hardly think this is the best place to discuss this." He kept his voice low. "Can it wait?"

She huffed out a breath, feeling stupid. "Of course.

I'm sorry. I guess it was being in the church that made me fly over here like this."

"Don't apologize," he said. "I'm the one who owes you a never-ending apology, and I fully intend to make up for the way I've hurt you, if it takes me the rest of my life." He gave her that crooked grin. "Now go on and float home in this rain. I'll come by when I get done with my paperwork."

"Okay." She floated home, all right, but not from the rain. She floated on the love she had for Lucas. Surely she couldn't be wrong about him this time. She saw it in his eyes, the way he felt about her: he did love her. And then something occurred to Miranda.

Lucas had loved her before. Just not enough to marry her. What if he felt the same way now?

She couldn't take it.

She busied herself with things that needed doing on the ranch, not letting the weather stop her. She wore her slicker and her cowboy hat, and worked on odds and ends she'd been meaning to get around to, like fixing the loose hinge on the barn door.

Belatedly, Miranda remembered she was supposed to meet Tori at the diner—just as Lucas pulled into the driveway. She watched him walk toward the house. He was so sexy.

"Over here," she called from the barn. Then she laughed as he took a pack of hot dogs from a plastic sack and fed a couple to Tuck and Smudge, who'd run over to bark at his truck the minute he'd pulled in.

"Hi." He grinned as he came into the barn. "I think they're starting to like me."

"I think they like the hot dogs," Miranda said. "If you really want them to like you, you'll have to find one of those hot dog suits and dress up in it. You know, like that guy in the TV commercial."

"I don't know about that. Then they might really go after me." Lucas set the bag on a shelf in the aisle, and pressed Miranda up against the wall. Bracing his hands on either side of her, he leaned forward and kissed her. "I wanted to do that so badly when you came into my office," he said. "You look cute with wet hair."

She laughed. "I wanted you to do that." She closed her eyes. "Kiss me again."

"Yes, ma'am."

He kissed her until Miranda knew they were about to end up right back where they had Saturday night.

She put one hand against his chest and gave Lucas a gentle push. "Hang on a minute, cowboy. We've got some talking to do."

"Talking?" He pretended to sulk. "I'd rather show you how much I love you than tell you."

"That's just it," Miranda said. "How much *do* you love me, Lucas?"

He took a deep breath. "Enough to ask you to marry me." He took hold of her hands and pressed them together in his. "Miranda, please trust me. Please give me another chance. Do you remember that I told you I'd never again make you a promise I wouldn't keep?"

"I remember."

"Well, I'm promising you now. If you walk down the aisle, I'll be there."

"Is that an official proposal?" Her heart raced, and her palms felt damp. She was still so afraid.

"You'd better believe it." He dropped to one knee. "Miranda, will you marry me? Will you spend the rest of your life as my wife? I promise I won't let you down this time. I love you. I was a stupid kid all those years ago." He kissed her hand, then stood and gathered her into his arms. "Say yes," he growled.

"I'll marry you, Lucas," she said softly, "but I won't walk down the aisle."

He looked taken aback. "What do you mean?"

"I can't go to the church again." The thought made her queasy. "There are too many bad memories there."

"Of course you can't," he said, kissing her softly. "I would never ask you to do that, Miranda. We'll figure out something else. I just need to know that you'll be my wife, and let me love you forever."

"I will."

He smiled and nuzzled her neck. "We've got a lot of making up to do."

She didn't make it to her lunch date with Tori.

LUCAS LAY BESIDE MIRANDA in her bedroom, watching her sleep. The clouds outside made it seem as if it were much later than twelve-thirty. She was finally going to be his wife. He had to think of something special for their wedding. A ceremony she'd never forget.

Hell. He was a cowboy. This wasn't exactly his area of expertise. Would Paige want to help him? Would she consider him good enough for her daughter, considering the past? There was only one way to find out.

Lucas got dressed, scrawled a note to Miranda and propped it on the pillow before heading outside. For once, Tuck and Smudge left him alone.

Well, hell. If the dogs had accepted him, everyone else ought to.

He pulled up at the Rocking W and took a deep breath. "Here goes nothin'."

He found Paige in the barn, trimming the hooves of a big red dun. She glanced up, surprised. "Sheriff. What are you doing here? Nothing's wrong, is it?"

"No, ma'am. For once, I think everything is A-OK." He took a deep breath. "I know I'm not your favorite person in the world, but I love your daughter."

"Well," she said, setting the gelding's hoof down, "you're not telling me anything I didn't already know." She straightened, one hand on her hip. "Lucas, you took a bullet for her. I guess I can't ask for much more than that."

He chuckled. "Yes, ma'am. But I thought you should know, I've asked Miranda to marry me."

"You gonna show up this time?" She softened the words with a smile.

"You'd better believe it."

"All right then. So, when's the wedding?"

"We haven't gotten quite that far," he said. "Miranda doesn't want to get married at the church."

"I suppose not. You looking for a place to hold the wedding?"

"Yeah." He gave the red dun a pat. "I'm not so good at this sort of thing. Can you help me out?"

"I reckon I can." She bent over the animal's hoof once more, then pointed the heavy metal file at him. "But if you don't show up, Lucas Blaylock, there won't be a single rock in this county you can hide under."

His lips twitched. "Yes, ma'am."

"And stop that damn ma'am stuff, like I told you before."

"Sure enough—Mom."

Paige peered at him from beneath the brim of her cowboy hat. "Now that's pushing it."

MIRANDA STOPPED BY THE Rocking W after her evening chores to visit with Shannon. The two dogs barked at her as she went in the house, then wagged their tails. Miranda petted them, happy to see the pups were already acting their part.

Shannon was in the kitchen, fixing supper.

"I told her to rest some more," Paige grumbled, "but she won't listen."

"Are you kidding?" Shannon grinned. "I'm so happy to be home, back to normal, I can't think of anything

I'd rather be doing right now." She chopped celery and glanced over her shoulder. "I hear there's a wedding in the making."

Miranda's jaw dropped. "Don't tell me Fae and Mae are psychic now, too."

Paige laughed. "Lucas came by to see me this afternoon."

"He did?"

"Looks like he's going to go through with it this time," Shannon said. "If not, Mom's already threatened him."

"He'd better," Miranda exclaimed. "What did he want, Mom?"

"A place to hold the ceremony. I thought about having it right here at the ranch, but Fae and Mae have the most beautiful garden in their backyard...I know you've seen it. I'm sure they won't mind."

"Oh, that would be perfect." Miranda sighed. "Is this really finally happening?"

"I'd say it is," Paige said. "Come here. I've got something for you."

Miranda followed her down the hall to her bedroom. Her mother's eyes danced. "I saved this, even though I wasn't sure I could ever look at it again." From the back of the closet, she pulled out a garment bag. "I didn't give it to you the first time around, because I was still too angry with your father to want you to have it."

She unzipped the bag and pulled out a lace-trimmed, satin wedding gown. The old-fashioned bodice was gathered, and a row of buttons ran from the neck to the waist. The sleeves were long and lacy, puffed at the shoulders just enough to be pretty, not tacky. The gown looked as though it could've come from the 1800s.

"It ought to fit you," Paige said. "I was about your size back then."

"Oh, Mom, it's gorgeous." Miranda ran her hand over the full skirt. "Why didn't you ever show this to me or Shannon?"

"Bad memories, I guess. But I think it's time we made some good ones." Paige sat on the edge of the bed. "I don't know what made your daddy run scared."

Miranda lifted a shoulder. "Probably the same thing that made Lucas run. He was young."

"Maybe so. But the difference is, Lucas grew up."

"It took him long enough."

Paige chuckled. "That's a fact. But I think he truly *has* grown up, Miranda. I think you've got yourself a winner there, honey. One well worth waiting for."

Miranda smiled. "I think so, too, Mom." She leaned over and hugged her. "I love the dress. I'd be proud to wear it."

"Then it's yours. But you have to pass it down to Shannon, if she ever decides to get married."

"I will." Miranda walked over to the doorway and called, "Hey, Shannon, come here. Mom has something to show you."

"I THINK THE ARCHWAY should go over there," Fae said, pointing.

"No, honey." Mae took her by the shoulders and turned her. "Over there." She gestured with one bejeweled hand. "It would be perfect over there, by the pond."

"Not if there are mosquitoes out!"

"Well, we'll just get some of those whatchamacallit candles."

"Citronella," Tori interjected helpfully.

Miranda's head spun. They'd been planning the August wedding—put together in a hurry because she and Lucas hadn't wanted to wait any longer—for the past few weeks. The local printer had done a rush order on invitations, and the florist where Lily Tate worked part-time had provided the white roses to decorate the archway, as well as the chairs they'd borrowed from the high school.

White roses, lace and all the beautiful flowers in Fae and Mae's garden. Who could ask for anything more?

Miranda stepped back and took it all in. The ceremony was going to be breathtaking. She'd even managed to talk Mac, Frank and Garrett into wearing suits for the day. They'd conceded only because she'd told them they could still wear their cowboy hats and boots.

Her mother had surprised her by whipping out an old sewing machine from her basement, and between her, Fae and Mae, they'd put together two bridesmaid dresses, and one for the matron of honor, matching the 1800s theme of Miranda's wedding gown.

The dresses were a rich teal-blue for the brides-maids, with a lighter sky-blue for the matron of honor. Miranda had agonized over choosing between Tori and Shannon for that position, until Fae had made a good suggestion.

"Ask your momma," she said. "She's suffered so much heartbreak in her life, honey. She deserves all the happiness God can throw her way. I know she'd be honored."

And Paige was. She'd burst into tears, and Miranda hadn't taken but a moment to decide she liked this new, emotional side of her mother.

Lucas had stepped back and let the women have at it. Beyond a fitting of his Western-cut tux, he wanted nothing more to do with the wedding arrangements. All he cared about was watching Miranda walk down that garden path to stand beside him, and he'd told her as much. She didn't really mind. Standing beside him was all she'd ever wanted.

"No mosquitoes," Miranda said. "Sorry, Mae. Fae wins this one." The twins had waged a friendly battle throughout the entire planning of the wedding, right down to the flavor of cake and the color of the roses.

But one thing the sisters agreed on—they couldn't be happier for Miranda, and they continually punctuated this fact by sniffling and dabbing at their eyes with tissues. Ever the drama queens.

"This is going to be so lovely," Mae said, conceding to Miranda on the placement of the archway. "Tori, when are you going to pick out a cowboy and get married?"

"Not anytime soon, thank you very much," her niece said, with a wink to Miranda. "Although I am bringing Jack McQuaid as my date." She lowered her voice so only Miranda could hear. "I think I'll get him drunk and take advantage of him."

Miranda laughed. Since half the town was invited to the wedding, the reception would be held at the Silver Spur.

"Works for me," Tori said. "I practically live there, anyway."

Fae and Mae were supplying all the food, which would be spread out buffet-style on tables covered with red-checkered clothes, with old-fashioned lanterns lighting each end. As a final touch, the local band, Wild Country, was going to play for them.

Through all the planning, all the fun of it, Miranda never once worried. She knew she was in good hands.

But on the day of her wedding, she turned into a mass of nerves. She sat in the guest bedroom of Fae and Mae's house, while Tori styled Miranda's hair and Shannon looked on.

"What if he changes his mind again?" Miranda asked for the umpteenth time.

Tori rolled her eyes. "I already told you. He's not about to change his mind. Not only does he love you, but he knows we'd string him up. And that would be the worst thing that could happen to the sheriff. Now sit still."

Once Tori was done with Miranda's hair, Shannon did her makeup. Finally, Miranda began to relax. The whole primping session took her back to their preteen years, when the two of them had experimented with their mother's makeup.

Paige came into the room just minutes before the ceremony was to start. "Oh, honey, you look like a picture." She leaned over and brushed a kiss against Miranda's forehead. "My baby, getting married."

"Excuse me," Shannon said. "I'm the baby of the family."

Miranda laughed. "Then you ought to thank me for blazing the trail for you." She stood and took a deep breath, gathering her skirt. "Well, here goes. Wish me luck."

"You won't need it," Tori said, as the four of them walked outside. "You're already the luckiest woman in the state of Montana." She nodded toward the end of the garden path. "That is one hot cowboy." She gave Miranda a wink, then took one of the small bouquets of flowers the bridesmaids were to carry from Paige, and started down the pathway.

Miranda was barely aware of the romantic country song that played over the loudspeakers in the garden, or of the photographer who snapped pictures of her and her attendants. Paige even had to give her a nudge when it was time to walk down the aisle, she was so focused on Lucas.

Miranda took her mother's hand and they walked down together.

Lucas stood beneath an archway of curling vines and white roses beside his deputies, his eyes locked on Miranda's. She felt her heart swell, felt a lump rise in her throat.

Of course he was there.

He held out his hand as she drew near. The expression on his face said she was his, now and forever. Lucas tucked her hand through his arm, and she lowered her bouquet of roses and baby's breath, standing beside him.

Partners.

The words they said to each other seemed almost an afterthought.

"Miranda, I promise to love you and honor you, and be your lifetime partner. And I promise to do my best to never give you cause to make me sleep on the couch."

Everyone chuckled, and even Pastor Hill smothered a smile.

"I'll do my best to keep you happy, now and always," Lucas added. "You're my wife, my love, my world." He slid a simple gold band onto her finger.

Miranda looked up at him, loving the way his ring felt on her hand. "Lucas, I never thought I'd get you here, but here we are. I promise to always love you, and honor you, and be your lifetime partner, as well. And I promise to be your friend and your lover and the woman who's waiting for you with a cold beer when you come home."

The cowboys among the rows of guests whistled and cheered. "Can't beat that!" someone called.

"But most of all," Miranda continued, "I'll be the woman who will grow old with you. Lucas Blaylock, I'm proud to be your wife." She slipped the gold band onto his finger.

Pastor Hill beamed. "Lucas...Miranda. I now pronounce you husband and wife. Miranda, you may kiss your groom."

"Gladly."

Cheers went up, and cowboy hats were tossed in the air. But Miranda barely paid attention.

She had eyes for only one cowboy.

And he had eyes only for her.

THEY LAY ON THE CREEK bank beneath the cottonwoods that night, with a bottle of champagne nearby. Miranda had locked Smudge and Tuck in the house with Happy.

"This isn't exactly the fancy hotel suite I'd had planned," Lucas said.

Miranda had made him cancel their reservations at the honeymoon suite in Billings.

"No, but it's so much better," she said. "And so

much more private." She looked up at the familiar blanket of stars. Centered almost perfectly above them, the moon was in its last quarter—a silver sliver that was somehow even more romantic than a full moon.

More darkness to snuggle in.

She would miss coming here, once Shannon moved in. Miranda hadn't had the heart to ask Lucas to give up his beautiful log home. Instead, they'd live there, though she'd still run her horse training business here. Shannon had been more than happy to buy out half of Bush Creek. She'd been saving for a ranch of her own for quite a while now.

Maybe Lucas and she could still sneak over to the creek on occasion, Miranda mused. For old times' sake.

She cuddled against his shoulder. They'd made love the minute they'd finished toasting one another as bride and groom. She looked down at the gold band on her finger. Lucas had promised her diamonds one day, and she'd told him he was all she really needed. Her diamond in the rough. He seemed satisfied with that.

He held up his hand, admiring his own wedding band. Then he folded his left hand over hers. "You know, I think I'm going to like being married."

"Yeah? Well I certainly hope so, because its way too late to back out now."

He rolled over and kissed her. "Not a chance of that." Then he grew serious. "How many kids do you want?"

"Kids?"

"Well, we're not getting any younger."

She gave him a playful shove. "Speak for yourself, cowboy." She kissed him, then mulled over his question with exaggerated concentration. "Hmm. I think two would be good."

"Just two." He kissed her. "How about three?"

"Maybe."

"Or four." He kissed her again.

"Only if you have that one." She kissed him back. "I think two or three is about all I can handle."

"We'll negotiate later." Lucas gathered her into his arms, pinning her to the blanket beneath them. "I say we start now."

"A honeymoon baby?" Miranda clicked her tongue. "What if she's born early? People will talk, you know."

"Let 'em talk," he said, kissing her again. "It'll give Fae and Mae something to run through their grapevine."

Miranda laughed softly, then pulled Lucas against her. She couldn't think of a better way to share their love.

A honeymoon baby sounded just right.

* * * * *

Every Life Has More
Than One Chapter

Award-winning author Stevi Mittman
delivers another hysterical mystery, featuring
Teddi Bayer, an irrepressible heroine, and
her to-die-for hero, Detective Drew Scoones.
After all, life on Long Island can be murder!

*Turn the page for a sneak peek at the warm and
funny fourth book,*
WHOSE NUMBER IS UP, ANYWAY?,
in the Teddi Bayer series,
by STEVI MITTMAN.
On sale August 7.

"Before redecorating a room, I always advise my
clients to empty it of everything but one chair.
Then I suggest they move that chair from place
to place, sitting in it, until the placement feels
right. Trust your instincts when deciding on furniture placement. Your room should "feel right.""
—TipsFromTeddi.com

Gut feelings. You know, that gnawing in the pit of
your stomach that warns you that you are about to
do the absolute stupidest thing you could do? Something that will ruin life as you know it?

I've got one now, standing at the butcher counter
in King Kullen, the grocery store in the same strip mall
as L.I. Lanes, the bowling alley–cum–billiard parlor
I'm in the process of redecorating for its "Grand
Opening."

I realize being in the wrong supermarket probably

doesn't sound exactly dire to you, but you aren't the one buying your father a brisket at a store your mother will somehow know isn't Waldbaum's.

And then, June Bayer isn't your mother.

The woman behind the counter has agreed to go into the freezer to find a brisket for me, since there aren't any in the case. There are packages of pork tenderloin, piles of spare ribs and rolls of sausage, but no briskets.

Warning number two, right? I should be so out of here.

But no, I'm still in the same spot when she comes back out, brisketless, her face ashen. She opens her mouth as if she is going to scream, but only a gurgle comes out.

And then she pinballs out from behind the counter, knocking bottles of Peter Luger Steak Sauce to the floor on her way, now hitting the tower of cans at the end of the prepared foods aisle and sending them sprawling, now making her way down the aisle, careening from side to side as she goes.

Finally, from a distance, I hear her shout, "He's deeeeeeaaaad! Joey's deeeeeaaaad."

My first thought is *You should always trust your gut*.

My second thought is that now, somehow, my mother will know I was in King Kullen. For weeks I will have to hear "What did you expect?" as though whenever you go to King Kullen someone turns up dead. And if the detective investigating the case turns out to be Detective Drew Scoones…well, I'll never hear the end of that from her, either.

She still suspects I murdered the guy who was found dead on my doorstep last Halloween just to get Drew back into my life.

Several people head for the butcher's freezer and I position myself to block them. If there's one thing I've learned from finding people dead—and the guy on my doorstep wasn't the first one—it's that the police get very testy when you mess with their murder scenes.

"You can't go in there until the police get here," I say, stationing myself at the end of the butcher's counter and in front of the Employees Only door, acting as if I'm some sort of authority. "You'll contaminate the evidence if it turns out to be murder."

Shouts and chaos. You'd think I'd know better than to throw the word *murder* around. Cell phones are flipping open and tongues are wagging.

I amend my statement quickly. "Which, of course, it probably isn't. Murder, I mean. People die all the time, and it's not always in hospitals or their own beds, or . . ." I babble when I'm nervous, and the idea of someone dead on the other side of the freezer door makes me very nervous.

So does the idea of seeing Drew Scoones again. Drew and I have this on-again, off-again sort of thing…that I kind of turned off.

Who knew he'd take it so personally when he tried

to get serious and I responded by saying we could talk about *us* tomorrow—and then caught a plane to my parents' condo in Boca the next day? In July. In the middle of a job.

For some crazy reason, he took that to mean that I was avoiding him and the subject of *us*.

That was three months ago. I haven't seen him since.

The manager, who identifies himself and points to his nameplate in case I don't believe him, says he has to go into *his cooler*. "Maybe Joey's not dead," he says. "Maybe he can be saved, and you're letting him die in there. Did you ever think of that?"

In fact, I hadn't. But I had thought that the murderer might try to go back in to make sure his tracks were covered, so I say that I will go in and check.

Which means that the manager and I couple up and go in together while everyone pushes against the doorway to peer in, erasing any chance of finding clean prints on that Employee Only door.

I expect to find carcasses of dead animals hanging from hooks, and maybe Joey hanging from one, too. I think it's going to be very creepy and I steel myself, only to find a rather benign series of shelves with large slabs of meat laid out carefully on them, along with boxes and boxes marked simply Chicken.

Nothing scary here, unless you count the body of a middle-aged man with graying hair sprawled faceup on the floor. His eyes are wideopen and unblinking. His shirt is stiff. His pants are stiff. His body is stiff. And his expression—you should forgive the pun—is frozen. Bill-the-manager crosses himself and stands mute while I pronounce the guy dead in a sort of *happy now?* tone.

"We should not be in here," I say, and he nods his head emphatically and helps me push people out of the doorway just in time to hear the police sirens and see the cop cars pull up outside the big store windows.

Bobbie Lyons, my partner in Teddi Bayer Interior Designs (and also my neighbor, my best friend and my private fashion police), and Mark, our carpenter (and my dogsitter, confidant and ego booster), rush in from next door. They beat the cops by a half step and shout out my name. People point in my direction.

After all the publicity that followed the unfortunate incident during which I shot my ex-husband, Rio Gallo, and then the subsequent murder of my first client—which I solved, I might add—it seems like the whole world, or at least all of Long Island, knows who I am.

Mark asks if I'm all right. (Did I remember to mention that the man is drop-dead-gorgeous-but-a-decade-too-young-for-me-yet-too-old-for-my-daughter-thank-god?) I don't get a chance to answer him because the police are quickly closing in on the store manager and me.

"The woman—" I begin telling the police. Then I have to pause for the manager to fill in her name, which he does: *Fran.*

I continue. "Right. Fran. Fran went into the freezer to get a brisket. A moment later she came out and screamed that Joey was dead. So I'd say she was the one who discovered the body."

"And you are…?" the cop asks me. It comes out a bit like who do I *think* I am, rather than who am I really.

"An innocent bystander," Bobbie, hair perfect, makeup just right, says, carefully placing her body between the cop and me.

"And she was just leaving," Mark adds. They each take one of my arms.

Fran comes into the inner circle surrounding the cops. In case it isn't obvious from the hairnet and bloodstained white apron with *Fran* embroidered on it, I explain that she was the butcher who was going for the brisket. Mark and Bobbie take that as a signal that I've done my job and they can now get me out of there. They twist around, with me in the middle, as if we're a Rockettes line, until we are facing away from the butcher counter. They've managed to propel me a few steps toward the exit when disaster—in the form of a Mazda RX7 pulling up at the loading curb—strikes.

Mark's grip on my arm tightens like a vise. "Too late," he says.

Bobbie's expletive is unprintable. "Maybe there's a back door," she suggests, but Mark is right. It's too late.

I've laid my eyes on Detective Scoones. And

while my gut is trying to warn me that my heart shouldn't go there, regions farther south are melting at just the sight of him.

"Walk," Bobbie orders me.

And I try to. Really.

Walk, I tell my feet. *Just put one foot in front of the other.*

I can do this because I know, in my heart of hearts, that, if Drew Scoones was still interested in me, he'd have gotten in touch with me after I returned from Boca. And he didn't.

Since he's a detective, Drew doesn't have to wear one of those dark blue Nassau County Police uniforms. Instead, he's got on jeans, a tight-fitting T-shirt and a tweedy sports jacket. If you think that sounds good, you should see him. Chiseled features, cleft chin, brown hair that's naturally a little sandy in the front, a smile that…well, that doesn't matter. He isn't smiling now.

He walks up to me, tucks his sunglasses into his breast pocket and looks me over from head to toe.

"Well, if it isn't Miss Cut and Run," he says. "Aren't you supposed to be somewhere in Florida or something?" He looks at Mark accusingly, as if he was covering for me when he told Drew I was gone.

"Detective Scoones?" one of the uniforms says. "The stiff's in the cooler and the woman who found him is over there." He jerks his head in Fran's direction.

Drew continues to stare at me.

You know how when you were young, your mother always told you to wear clean underwear in case you were in an accident? And how, a little further on, she told you not to go out in hair rollers because you never knew who you might see—or who might see you? And how now your best friend says she wouldn't be caught dead without makeup and suggests you shouldn't either?

Okay, today, *finally,* in my overalls and Converse sneakers, I get it.

I brush my hair out of my eyes. "Well, I'm back," I say. As if he hasn't known my exact whereabouts. The man is a detective, for heaven's sake. "Been back awhile."

Bobbie has watched the exchange and apparently decided she's given Drew all the time he deserves. "And we've got work to do, so…" she says, grabbing my arm and giving Drew a little two-fingered wave goodbye.

As I back up a foot or two, the store manager sees his chance and places himself in front of Drew, trying to get his attention. Maybe what makes Drew such a good detective is his ability to focus.

Only what he's focusing on is me.

"Phone broken? Carrier pigeon died?" he asks me, taking in Fran, the manager, the meat counter and that Employees Only door, all without taking his eyes off me.

Mark tries to break the spell. "We've got work to

do there, you've got work to do here, Scoones," Mark says to him, gesturing toward next door. "So it's back to the alley for us."

Drew's lip twitches. "You working the alley now?" he says.

"If you'd like to follow me," Bill-the-manager, clearly exasperated, says to Drew—who doesn't respond. It's as if waiting for my answer is all he has to do.

So, fine. "You knew I was back," I say.

The man has known my whereabouts every hour of the day for as long as I've known him. And my mother's not the only one who won't buy that he "just happened" to answer this particular call. In fact, I'm willing to bet my children's lunch money that he's taken every call within ten miles of my home since the day I got back.

And now he's gotten lucky.

"*You* could have called *me*," I say.

"You're the one who said *tomorrow* for our talk and then flew the coop, chickie," he says. "I figured the ball was in your court."

"Detective?" the uniform says. "There's something you ought to see in here."

Drew gives me a look that amounts to *in or out?*

He could be talking about the investigation, or about our relationship.

Bobbie tries to steer me away. Mark's fists are balled. Drew waits me out, knowing I won't be able to resist what might be a murder investigation.

Finally he turns and heads for the cooler.

And, like a puppy dog, I follow.

Bobbie grabs the back of my shirt and pulls me to a halt.

"I'm just going to show him something," I say, yanking away.

"Yeah," Bobbie says, pointedly looking at the buttons on my blouse. The two at breast level have popped. "That's what I'm afraid of."

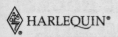

HARLEQUIN®

American ROMANCE®

TEXAS LEGACIES: THE CARRIGANS

Get to the Heart of a Texas Family

WITH

THE RANCHER NEXT DOOR
by
Cathy Gillen Thacker

She'll Run The Ranch—And Her Life—Her Way!

On her alpaca ranch in Texas, Rebecca encounters
constant interference from Trevor McCabe, the
bossy rancher next door. Rebecca becomes very
friendly with Vince Owen, her other neighbor and
Trevor's archrival from college. Trevor's problem
is convincing Rebecca that he is on her side, and
aware of Vince's ulterior motives. But Trevor has
fallen for her in the process....

On sale July 2007

www.eHarlequin.com   HAR75173

REQUEST YOUR FREE BOOKS!
2 FREE NOVELS PLUS 2 FREE GIFTS!

HARLEQUIN®

Super Romance®

Exciting, emotional, unexpected!

YES! Please send me 2 FREE Harlequin Superromance® novels and my 2 FREE gifts. After receiving them, if I don't wish to receive any more books, I can return the shipping statement marked "cancel." If I don't cancel, I will receive 6 brand-new novels every month and be billed just $4.69 per book in the U.S., or $5.24 per book in Canada, plus 25¢ shipping and handling per book and applicable taxes, if any*. That's a savings of close to 15% off the cover price! I understand that accepting the 2 free books and gifts places me under no obligation to buy anything. I can always return a shipment and cancel at any time. Even if I never buy another book from Harlequin, the two free books and gifts are mine to keep forever.

135 HDN EEX7 336 HDN EEYK

Name   (PLEASE PRINT)

Address   Apt.

City   State/Prov.   Zip/Postal Code

Signature (if under 18, a parent or guardian must sign)

Mail to the **Harlequin Reader Service®**:
IN U.S.A.: P.O. Box 1867, Buffalo, NY 14240-1867
IN CANADA: P.O. Box 609, Fort Erie, Ontario L2A 5X3

Not valid to current Harlequin Superromance subscribers.

Want to try two free books from another line?
Call 1-800-873-8635 or visit www.morefreebooks.com.

* Terms and prices subject to change without notice. NY residents add applicable sales tax. Canadian residents will be charged applicable provincial taxes and GST. This offer is limited to one order per household. All orders subject to approval. Credit or debit balances in a customer's account(s) may be offset by any other outstanding balance owed by or to the customer. Please allow 4 to 6 weeks for delivery.

Your Privacy: Harlequin is committed to protecting your privacy. Our Privacy Policy is available online at www.eHarlequin.com or upon request from the Reader Service. From time to time we make our lists of customers available to reputable firms who may have a product or service of interest to you. If you would prefer we not share your name and address, please check here. ☐

HSR07

EVERLASTING LOVE™

Every great love has a story to tell™

*A love story that distance and time
has never dimmed.*

While remodeling her home, April
finds some old love letters addressed
to Norma Marsh. Tracking down the
owner, now in her eighties, brings to the
surface secrets Norma has kept from her
grandson Quinn, about a love close to
her heart. A love April begins to understand
as she starts to fall for Quinn…

Look for

by

Roz Denny Fox

On sale August 2007.

COMING NEXT MONTH

#1434 LOVE, BY GEORGE • Debra Salonen
You, Me & the Kids

Man's best friend turns matchmaker when two single parents intent on avoiding romance find they can't avoid each other—thanks to a rambunctious Great Dane named George.

#1435 THE MAN FROM HER PAST • Anna Adams
Welcome to Honesty

Cassie Warne is bringing a secret home to Honesty—a daughter she has never told anyone she had. Cassie is returning only to care for her ill father; she doesn't plan to stay. And she hopes she can avoid her ex, Van. But Van has other ideas.

#1436 GOOD WITH CHILDREN • Margot Early

Rory Gorenzi's employment history is a little erratic, so she's determined to keep her current job—teaching skiing and avalanche safety at her father's Colorado mountain school. She's always been good with children, which makes her the ideal teacher for widower Seamus Lee's four kids. *And the ideal woman for him?*

#1437 NANNY MAKES THREE • Joan Kilby
Single Father

Gregory Finch is a single lawyer juggling legalese, a young daughter…and a pig farm. He needs help. Which Melissa Cummings could provide, except that she's too busy looking for a higher purpose in life to be a nanny. Until, that is, she realizes it's the ideal cover so she can help the runaway hiding in Gregory's barn.

#1438 MAYBE, BABY • Terry McLaughlin
Bright Lights, Big Sky

Film producer Burke Elliot arrives in Montana on a mission: to convince actress Nora Daniels to sign a contract and return to Hollywood. And nothing he encounters can stop him. Except…a blizzard that traps him in a cabin with the actress who's turning him inside out and the baby who's wrapping him around her tiny finger.

#1439 THE FAMILY SOLUTION • Bobby Hutchinson

Bella Jane Monroe's life took a dramatic turn for the worse on her thirty-seventh birthday when she woke up to find her husband had abandoned her and their kids. Stuck with a failing business, she draws inspiration from the most unlikely source—the real estate agent trying to get her house.